"So, did yo‸‸‸‸‸‸‸‸‸‸‸‸‸‸‸‸‸‸‸‸‸‸‸‸‸?" Jessica asked.

"I couldn't‸‸‸‸‸‸‸‸‸‸‸‸‸‸‸‸‸‸‸‸‸‸u already knew t‸‸‸‸‸‸‸‸‸‸‸‸‸‸‸‸‸‸‸‸d is filled for tomorrow. A certain Ms. J. Wakefield has scheduled an all-day lesson."

"Oh, that's right," Jessica said. "I forgot about that. I thought a whole day of intense work, one on one, would be just the ticket to improve my skiing. I've always wanted to build up my speed, you know."

"You're already the *fastest* girl around," Lila said acidly. "But you're crazy if you think you're going to get Lucas all to yourself tomorrow. We're sharing that all-day lesson. Period."

"I told you that all's fair in love and war," she reminded Lila. "It looks to me as if the Battle of Snow Mountain has begun. And you just lost a round."

. Lila's face looked as if it were carved out of ice.

FALLING
FOR LUCAS

Written by
Kate William

Created by
FRANCINE PASCAL

BANTAM BOOKS
NEW YORK · TORONTO · LONDON · SYDNEY · AUCKLAND

FALLING FOR LUCAS
A BANTAM BOOK : 0 553 50465 7

Originally published in U.S.A. by Bantam Books

First publication in Great Britain

PRINTING HISTORY
Bantam edition published 1997

Conceived by Francine Pascal

Produced by Daniel Weiss Associates, Inc,
33 West 17th Street, New York, NY 10011

Bantam Books are published by Transworld Publishers Ltd,
61–63 Uxbridge Road, Ealing, London W5 5SA,
in Australia by Transworld Publishers (Australia) Pty Ltd,
15–25 Helles Avenue, Moorebank, NSW 2170,
and in New Zealand by Transworld Publishers (NZ) Ltd,
3 William Pickering Drive, Albany, Auckland.

Printed and bound in Great Britain by
Cox & Wyman Ltd, Reading, Berkshire.

To Steven Lev Groopman

Chapter 1

A pearl of chocolate-marshmallow ice cream slid down the outside of Jessica Wakefield's sundae dish as she stood in the bustling dining room of Casey's Ice Cream Parlor on Thursday afternoon. She rescued the dripping ice cream with her tongue.

Her best friend, Lila Fowler, arched her perfectly tweezed eyebrows. "That's really gauche, Jess."

"Well, excuse me for living," Jessica replied. "But my other hand is full of shopping bags. Besides, it's a lot less gauche than having ice cream smears all over my silk blouse."

"*Your* blouse?" Lila asked, eyeing the aqua blouse that matched the color of Jessica's eyes. "I thought that one was your sister's."

Jessica shrugged. "My blouse, Elizabeth's . . . what does it matter?" she said glibly. "It's share and

1

share alike when you're identical twins. Speaking of Liz, do you see her anywhere? She said she'd meet us at four o'clock. It must be four by now."

Lila pointed. "She's in the corner, with that geek Enid," she said with a sniff. "And we're late. It's four thirty."

Sure enough, Jessica's twin sister was sitting in the corner booth of the popular ice cream shop, across from her best friend, Enid Rollins.

Like Jessica, Elizabeth was five foot six and slender, with wholesome good looks. The sixteen-year-old twins had blond hair, heart-shaped faces, and big blue-green eyes. But Jessica played up her appearance with carefully applied makeup and the trendiest fashions. Elizabeth preferred a more natural look, with classic, preppy clothes. That day she was wearing her hair pulled back in a ponytail. *Practical, but decidedly unsexy,* Jessica thought with a sigh.

Even if their hair and makeup had been identical, people who knew the Wakefields would have little trouble telling them apart. Both twins were among the most popular girls in the junior class at Sweet Valley High, but people liked them for different reasons. Vivacious Jessica, the life of every party, liked being the center of attention. Flirting, gossiping, and cheerleading were among her favorite activities. Quiet, sensitive Elizabeth spent her time on more serious pursuits, such as writing in her journal, helping her friends with personal problems, and working for the school newspaper.

And Elizabeth could always be counted on to be punctual—unlike Jessica, who refused even to wear a watch. That afternoon in the ice cream parlor was typical.

"A half hour late is no big deal," Jessica said, whipping her head to one side to toss back her long, carefully tousled hair. "Elizabeth and Enid always expect me to be late. I wouldn't want to disappoint them."

"I don't know why you let Elizabeth hang out with somebody who's so uncool," Lila remarked as they walked toward Elizabeth and Enid's table. "I would be mortified if anyone related to me had a best friend like Enid Rollins."

"Liz may have gotten all the brains in the family," Jessica said, thinking ruefully of her sister's straight-A report cards. "But I'm a much better judge of character than she is."

"You certainly have more sophisticated taste in best friends," Lila said, smoothing her own silky brown hair. "Can you believe that beaded sweater Enid is wearing? Nobody's wearing fifties fashions this year. It's just too retro."

"I know," Jessica agreed. "But Enid is Elizabeth's best friend, so let's try to be nice to her."

3

Elizabeth waved. "Hey, Jessica!" she called, sliding over to make room for her sister. "What took you guys so long?" As she sipped her milk shake, she eyed the shopping bags in Jessica's hand. "Or should I ask?"

"Oh, we were just picking up a few necessities for the trip tomorrow," Jessica said with a shrug.

"Hello, Enid," Lila said in a syrupy voice. "What a pretty sweater! That retro look is very in."

"Thanks, Lila," Enid said uncertainly, moving her half-eaten hot-fudge sundae to make room for Lila. Enid didn't like Jessica's best friend any more than Lila liked Enid. But Jessica knew they were willing to tolerate each other occasionally for the sake of the twins. At least Enid was smart enough to ignore Lila's haughty tone. "So are you two all ready to hit the ski slopes?" Enid asked.

Jessica shook her head. "Not yet. I found a totally cool pair of sunglasses at Bibi's," she said, holding up a small bag. "But I still haven't picked out the sexiest snow-bunny outfit in the mall."

"Second sexiest," Lila corrected her, daintily dipping her spoon into a dish of her favorite ice-cream flavor, Million-Dollar Mocha. "The sexiest one will be for me."

"No way!" Jessica countered.

"Way!" Lila insisted. "I mean, it's not like you could even afford it."

"The sexiest doesn't always have to mean the most expensive," Jessica pointed out. "Just because you're a millionaire—"

"Face it, Jess," Lila interrupted. "You can't compete."

Jessica forced herself to smile. "Not financially," she agreed. "But when it comes to style—"

Enid and Elizabeth looked at each other and burst out laughing.

"You two are so competitive!" Elizabeth said. "Can't you work *together* on something for a change?"

"Competitive?" Lila asked, her brown eyes wide and innocent. "*Moi?* Honestly, Liz, I don't have to prove anything to Jessica or anyone else in Sweet Valley."

"Neither do I," Jessica said. "Though, of course, there's nothing wrong with a little healthy competition between friends now and then."

"Nothing at all," Lila agreed. "Though in a way we will be working together this week. I mean, with me *and* Jessica as the sexiest female skiers in Colorado, nobody else is going to have a chance at the best-looking male ski instructors."

"Story of my life," Enid said with a sigh. She pushed a stray lock of wavy reddish brown hair out of her eyes. "Glamorous types like you two always get the guys," she complained. "No good-looking ski instructor will come near me—unless I tumble

5

down the mountain and he's forced to rescue me."

"Don't you dare try it!" Elizabeth said. "You're too good a skier for that—probably the best skier going on this trip. And stop selling yourself short. You're an interesting, attractive person, and any guy would be lucky to get you—"

Jessica thought she would throw up if she had to hear another word. Elizabeth's pep talks to Enid could get pretty sickening. "Want to see my new sunglasses?" Jessica interrupted. Lila sighed gratefully.

"Where are you shopping next?" Enid asked.

"Lisette's," Lila said. "Amy Sutton said they just got in a new shipment of ski stuff, in time for spring break."

"Why isn't Amy going on this trip?" Enid asked. "I thought the three of you were like the Three Musketeers."

"More like the Three Stooges," Elizabeth said.

"Ha, ha," Jessica replied to her sister. She turned to Enid. "Amy's failing French," she explained. "Her mother said she has to stay home and study."

"Amy's not the only one who's failing French," Lila reminded Jessica.

"Yeah, but there's one very important difference between Amy's French grade and my own," Jessica said. "Amy's mother knows about hers."

"Jessica!" cried Elizabeth.

6

"Don't worry about it," Jessica assured her. "I've got everything under control. Ms. Dalton said I could take a make-up test after we get back from Colorado. I'll pass somehow. I always do."

"Jessica, you're amazing," Enid said, pushing away her empty dish. "But Liz and I had better get going. I have to buy a new suitcase in time to go home and fill it with stuff for tomorrow."

"You want to hear something really sick?" Jessica said, leaning forward conspiratorially. "Elizabeth finished packing two days ago!"

"What's wrong with that?" Elizabeth asked. "Now I can go out with Todd tonight while you're scrambling around trying to find clothes that aren't too wrinkled to bring along."

Jessica shrugged. "That's no problem," she said to Elizabeth with a grin. "There are usually plenty of ironed clothes in *your* room!" She turned to Lila. "Besides, how much fun could a date with Todd Wilkins be? He's a hunk, but he's a boring hunk."

Despite her playful tone, Jessica suddenly felt depressed. Talking about her sister's steady boy-friend made her remember that she didn't have one anymore. She had recently broken up with Ken Matthews, the star quarterback for the Sweet Valley High Gladiators, after she fell desperately in love with Christian Gorman. But her relationship with Christian had ended in tragedy.

7

"Wow, Liz," Lila said. "I hadn't even thought of it before. But you and Todd will be together in Colorado for a whole week—with no parents around! Ooh-la-la!"

"Don't be silly," Elizabeth said. "I'm sharing a room with Enid, and Todd is sharing with Winston. Besides, you know the trip is chaperoned. Mr. Collins and Ms. Jacobi will be there the whole time, making sure everybody behaves."

Lila shook her head. "You and Todd are hopelessly straight!" she said. "A week in the mountains will be entirely wasted on you two."

Jessica sighed, still thinking of Christian. It would be good to get away from school and out of town for a while. Jessica thought Sweet Valley was the prettiest town in southern California. But it was small and full of memories—and lately most of them were sad memories. Christian was dead, and it was time for Jessica to get on with her life. A week on the ski slopes would help her feel like her old, high-spirited self again.

"This trip is going to be a fresh start," she decided.

Jessica didn't realize she had whispered the words aloud until her sister looked at her curiously.

"What did you say?" Elizabeth asked.

"This shopping trip is about to get a fresh start," Jessica said quickly, grinning. "Now that we've fortified ourselves with ice cream, it's time to hit the stores again. Two very sexy snow-bunny outfits are out there somewhere, and they've got my name and Lila's all over them!"

"I feel sorry for all those handsome ski instructors," Enid remarked as they slid out of the booth. "You two will be harder to hold back than an avalanche!"

"You should have heard Jessica this afternoon," Elizabeth said to Todd as they sat in his black BMW in front of the Wakefields' split-level home that evening. "She and Lila were going on and on about how they were going to buy the sexiest ski suits in the mall and then try to date the best-looking ski instructors on Snow Mountain."

Todd laughed. "Those poor ski instructors," he said. "Will Jess and Lila ever grow up and realize how much better it is to have a meaningful, long-term relationship?"

He leaned over and kissed Elizabeth on the lips. As usual, Todd's kiss sent tingles through her entire body. She shivered deliciously and twirled her fingers in his dark, wavy hair. "Mmmm," she murmured. "Does that mean I don't have to buy hot-pink spandex ski pants in order to get your attention this weekend on the slopes?"

Todd's eyebrows shot up. "Spandex, huh?" he asked speculatively. "You know, that might not be a bad idea—"

9

Elizabeth swatted him playfully on the head. "Thanks a lot!"

"I'm kidding! I'm kidding!" he insisted, shielding his face. "You look great without any spandex ski pants!"

Elizabeth's eyes widened. "Todd! Did you hear what you just said?"

"Maybe you'd better kiss me quickly so I don't have time to put my foot in my mouth again," he suggested. In the light from a streetlamp, his chocolate brown eyes twinkled.

Elizabeth tilted her head up to meet Todd's lips. His hands began moving in slow, delicious circles on her back. And once again Elizabeth felt herself melting in the warmth of his kiss. Why did he have to be so darn irresistible? It was too easy to forget herself when they were alone together. Elizabeth pulled away.

"We don't have to stop just yet," Todd said in a breathless voice.

"Yes, we do," Elizabeth whispered, feeling strangely shy. "You know it, too." Her heart was pounding so loudly that she was sure Todd could hear it.

He nodded. "I guess you're right," he agreed reluctantly. He sat back in the leather seat, his arm still around Elizabeth, and pulled her close, so her head rested on his shoulder. "But next week is going

10

to be different, Liz!" he promised. "This ski trip will be a great chance for us to spend some time alone."

Elizabeth smiled up at him. "That sounds nice," she said. "But remember, we're not exactly going to be alone. I'm sharing a room with Enid, and you're sharing with Winston."

Todd grinned. "Don't you worry about Winston Egbert," he said. "My roomie and I have a system worked out. Trust me—you and I will have plenty of time to ourselves."

The afternoon sunlight threw shifting shadows across the suburban streets on Friday as Jessica drove the twins' Jeep toward Sweet Valley High. School was out for a whole week. After a brief stop at home to drop off their books and collect their luggage, the girls were on their way back to the high school to catch the chartered bus to Snow Mountain.

Jessica yawned. "I still don't see why they made us go to school today," she complained. "If we'd left on spring break this morning, we would be practically to Colorado by now. And we wouldn't have to sleep on a moving bus tonight."

"Even if we'd been driving since nine this morning, we wouldn't even be close to Colorado by now," Elizabeth said. "But we might be at the Utah border."

"Whatever," Jessica said with a shrug. "Life's

11

too short to keep track of geography."

"Anyhow, you know we can't afford another night in a hotel room," Elizabeth continued. "As it is, the reservations we already made for this trip are going to clean out both our savings accounts."

Jessica laughed. "And an advance on my allowance that should keep me broke for the next three decades."

"Besides," Elizabeth added, "with your grades in French class lately, the last thing you need is to skip a day of school. You should have brought your French book along to study those verb conjugations when you have some spare time this week."

"You're too uptight, Liz," Jessica chastised her. "What's a grade, really? It's just a letter on a piece of paper. Big deal. And who in their right mind would study over spring break?"

Elizabeth laughed. "OK, OK! I'd give you more big-sisterly advice, but you always seem to squeak through somehow. But right now you look exhausted. How late were you up last night?"

"Too late," Jessica said with a shrug. "But I had to pack, didn't I?"

"You could have packed ahead of time, the way I did."

"We can't all be perfect, like you," Jessica said, rolling her eyes. "But I thought you weren't going to give me any more big-sisterly advice."

"So I lied," Elizabeth said. "What good is being born four minutes before you if I can't lord it over you now and then?"

Jessica raised her eyebrows. "Now and then?" she exclaimed. "Try every minute of every day."

"No way!" Elizabeth objected. "I'm not all *that* bossy."

"Yes, you are," Jessica said good-naturedly. "But that's OK. I'm used to it. I'd hardly recognize you if you weren't telling me what to do every three minutes."

"I do not tell you what to do!" Elizabeth protested as Jessica pulled up at a stoplight. "Make a right turn at this intersection, Jess," she added. "It'll be faster than our usual way, now that it's rush hour."

Jessica gave her sister what she hoped was a withering gaze and continued straight through the light.

Elizabeth opened her mouth to protest but then stopped herself. She laughed instead. "Oops," she said. "I guess I do kind of tell you what to do."

"That's a blinding flash of the obvious," Jessica said. "You're not planning on playing Attila the Twin all week on the ski slopes, are you?"

"As long as you're not about to hurl yourself face-first down the side of the mountain, I'll try to keep my big-sisterly advice to myself," Elizabeth agreed. "Even Attila needs a vacation."

"You never saw my new snow-bunny outfit!"

Jessica reminded her. "This outfit is hot enough to melt the snow for ten feet around me! I wanted to show you last night, but you were out with Todd by the time Lila dropped me off."

"I suppose Lila found something equally as devastating?" Elizabeth asked.

"Hers is more expensive," Jessica admitted. "It's cornflower blue—only she calls it *French* blue—with real rabbit-fur lining in the hood."

Elizabeth grimaced. "Yuck. I would never wear fur."

"I'd wear it in a minute if I could afford it," Jessica admitted. "But I don't need rabbit to be a snow bunny."

"A snow bunny, Jess?" Elizabeth asked, her tone horrified. "Don't you see how that kind of language just supports the sexist stereotypes that women—"

"Lighten up, Liz," Jessica urged. "Worrying about things like that gives you wrinkles. Besides, I was telling you about my new ski suit! The pants are purple spandex, and the parka is color-blocked, purple and hot pink!"

"It sounds as if you'll have to beat off the sexy ski instructors with your ski poles," Elizabeth said in a dry voice.

"Why beat them off?" Jessica asked, mystified. "The more the merrier."

Elizabeth's face turned serious. "The person I'm really worried about is Enid."

Jessica laughed. "You're worried that Enid's going to have to beat off sexy ski instructors? I think not."

"Don't be mean!" Elizabeth protested. "Enid's a very attractive girl. But she's been a little depressed ever since she and Hugh Grayson broke up. She would really like to meet someone to have a good time with next week."

"In her dreams," Jessica said.

"That's a mean thing to say!"

Jessica shrugged. "Sorry. I wasn't trying to be nasty. Well, not completely. Enid's not ugly or anything. She just doesn't do much with herself—kind of like you."

Elizabeth folded her arms across her chest. "Thanks a lot," she said.

"Oh, you know what I mean," Jessica said. "You're naturally gorgeous. You can get away with nothing but a touch of lip gloss and a little mascara. Enid's cute enough, I guess. But she's not a knockout. And she doesn't do anything to call attention to herself. She kind of fades into the background."

"And she can be shy around people she doesn't know well," Elizabeth said. "Enid doesn't have a lot of confidence."

For good reason, Jessica wanted to reply. But she clamped her mouth shut on the words. They might be true, but there was no need to antagonize her twin. Next to bossiness, she thought, Elizabeth's most annoying trait was a tenacious kind of loyalty to the people she cared about—*at least,* Jessica admitted, *it's annoying when Elizabeth uses it for anyone but me!*

"There's the bus to Snow Mountain!" she said instead, pointing toward the school parking lot, half a block away. "And there's the whole gang, waiting to get on—including a certain tall, dark, and handsome young stud getting out of a black BMW. Lila's right about you and Todd—all alone for a whole week, with no parents! Don't do anything I wouldn't do!"

Elizabeth raised her eyebrows at the last remark but let it slide. "Jessica," she said instead, "don't you start that, too! You know that my relationship with Todd is about a lot more than hormones."

"Of course," Jessica said seriously. "He loves you only for your mind. C'mon, Liz. Grow up! Guys couldn't care less about your mind. Do you honestly think Todd would love you if your hair looked like a bird's nest and you weighed three hundred pounds?"

"I never said that he doesn't like the way I look. But that's not the only thing our relationship is based on. Todd respects me."

Jessica hooted. "He's a guy, Liz. And if there's

one thing I'm an expert on, it's guys. Believe me, they're all pretty much alike."

"Well, you're not an expert on Todd! He's a lot deeper than some of the Neanderthals you've dated. He's interested in someone who's a good companion. Someone he can carry on an intelligent conversation with. Someone who shares his interests—"

"Someone he's going to be alone with in the mountains for spring break, with no parents for a thousand miles!" Jessica said gleefully.

"We'll hardly be alone," Elizabeth reminded her. "Sixteen kids will be on this trip, along with two chaperones. But even if we did manage to find some time alone in the mountains, Todd's not the type to take advantage of the situation."

"Ha!" Jessica snorted. "You just wait and see."

Todd turned awkwardly in bed—actually a bus seat that folded out into a bunk, like all the others on the chartered bus. He squinted to read his watch in the dark. It was after midnight, and the other passengers seemed to be asleep. Todd was tired, but his eyelids just wouldn't stay shut. He didn't even know what was keeping him up. The only sounds were Mr. Collins's soft snoring from his bunk in the very back of the bus, mingled with the low whine of the tires on Interstate 15.

He untwisted his sleeping bag from around his body, sat up, and scanned the rows of sleepers. He and the other boys were stretched out on the bunks in the back half of the bus; the girls were in the front. Directly across the aisle from Todd, Winston lay sprawled on his back, his mouth wide open. In the bunk in front of Winston's, all that could be seen of Neil Freemount was a shock of light-colored hair sticking out from the top of his sleeping bag.

Todd turned to look toward the front of the bus. He knew exactly which bunk was Elizabeth's: the last one on the left side in the girls' section. And he was almost sure he could see a glimmer of her golden hair, shining like a night light. Suddenly Todd knew exactly why he couldn't sleep. He had to be with Elizabeth, even if it was only for a minute or two.

Slowly Todd eased himself out of his sleeping bag. He winced as his bare feet touched the cold floor of the aisle. He paused, listening for the gentle snoring of Mr. Collins from the back of the bus.

Good, Todd almost said aloud. The English teacher was still asleep. It wouldn't do to have a chaperone catch him stealing toward his girlfriend's bed in the middle of the night—even if all he wanted was to feel Elizabeth in his arms and maybe give her a good-night kiss. After that, he was sure, he'd be able to sleep.

Todd padded silently toward Elizabeth's bunk. He glanced toward the bus driver up ahead, suddenly afraid that the woman would feel some obligation to wake the chaperones—Ms. Jacobi's bunk was within easy reach, directly behind the driver's seat. But the driver's eyes were on the road; she seemed oblivious to Todd's stealthy movements in the aisle.

At Elizabeth's bunk, Todd reached a tentative finger toward a lock of blond hair that spilled out over the edge of her sleeping bag. He smiled. Elizabeth's hair was so beautiful. Elizabeth was so beautiful. He ached to hold her against his chest— to feel her lips on his. Her sleeping bag was practically up to her chin; the air on the bus was a little cool. Carefully Todd climbed onto the bunk and lay down beside her. He enveloped his girlfriend in his arms and felt his body relax at her familiar warmth, even through the thick fiberfill of her sleeping bag.

For a moment Elizabeth's lips parted slightly as she snuggled against the collar of his flannel pajamas. In the darkness, he saw her eyelids flutter prettily.

Elizabeth stiffened abruptly. Her eyes flew open.

"Todd?" she asked aloud. Her voice lowered to a hiss. *"What the heck do you think you're doing?"*

19

Suddenly her hands were pushing against his chest—pushing him away.

Todd was glad for the darkness of the bus. It hid the blush that he could feel spreading over his face. Maybe this hadn't been such a good idea after all. "It's all right," he whispered into her ear. "I didn't mean to startle you. I, uh, just wanted to fall asleep in your arms."

"Are you out of your mind?" Elizabeth whispered back, sitting up quickly. A passing flash of light showed outrage in her eyes. "Here? On a bus full of people? What were you thinking?"

Suddenly another voice boomed out over the whining of the wheels. "Todd Wilkins, return to your own bunk now!" commanded Mr. Collins from the back of the bus.

Elizabeth fell back onto the bunk, mortified.

"Sorry," Todd whispered. He jumped from the bunk and leaned over to give her a quick peck on the cheek. But Elizabeth pulled away.

"Todd!" came the chaperone's voice again. Todd had never heard the English teacher sound so stern.

"We'll talk in the morning," Todd promised Elizabeth in a low voice. Then he scooted down the aisle.

Back in his own bunk, Todd lay staring at the ceiling of the bus, feeling the vibrations of the road through his body. He wondered how many of his classmates had been awakened by the incident. If everyone knew about it in the morning, Elizabeth would hate him forever.

Todd sighed. So far, this was not the romantic ski trip he had envisioned.

Chapter 2

On Saturday at nine o'clock in the morning, Elizabeth and Enid sat in a rest-stop diner near Grand Junction, Colorado. Elizabeth waved to their friend Olivia Davidson, who was just entering the room. As usual, Elizabeth smiled at the colorful outfit that artistic Olivia had put together. Compared to Elizabeth's own Sweet Valley University sweatshirt and jeans, Olivia's hand-painted shirt and leggings were loaded with flair.

"Olivia!" she called. "Come sit with Enid and me!"

Olivia's brown curls bobbed as she nodded, smiling. "Thanks for the invite!" she said as she slid into the booth next to Enid. "I was afraid I'd end up eating breakfast with Caroline Pearce this morning. It's bad enough that I'm stuck rooming with her all week—" She stopped, blushing.

"Gosh, I'm sorry. I must sound like a real snob."

Enid laughed. "No, you don't," she told Olivia. "We know exactly where you're coming from."

"Caroline means well," Elizabeth said, "but she tries too hard to get people to like her. She'd be a lot easier to take if she would just relax."

Olivia nodded. "Well, whatever her reasons for it, hours of mindless gossip about people I couldn't care less about is not my idea of stimulating conversation. On the other hand, I kind of feel responsible for her, since she's my roommate. I shouldn't leave her to eat breakfast all by herself."

"Don't worry," Enid said. "She seems to have hooked up with Jessica and Lila for now."

Sure enough, the small, red-haired junior was close on the heels of Jessica and Lila, who seemed to enjoy having an adoring audience. They were strolling through the restaurant, obviously trying to choose the best table for seeing and being seen.

"It works for me," Olivia replied. "Caroline will have more fun with them, anyhow. Jess and Lila are better sources of gossip than the three of us any day."

"Usually they are," Elizabeth said glumly. "But after Todd's idiotic maneuver last night, I'm sure I'm providing plenty of raw material for Caroline's rumor mill this morning."

"Unlike me," Enid said. "The only time she'd

have reason to talk about me is if her usual crowd of listeners needed help falling asleep. Do you know how long it's been since I've even had a real date?"

Elizabeth shrugged. "I'd be happy to lend you Todd for a while," she said dryly. "I'm so mad at him I can hardly see straight."

"Don't worry about it, Liz," Olivia said. "Everyone knows that you and Todd aren't really like that."

"At the moment, I'm not even sure that Todd isn't really like that!" Elizabeth complained. "I wonder how long I'll have to put up with people snickering about it."

Olivia smiled encouragingly. "Not long," she said. "People will joke about it for a day or two. But nobody will actually believe that anything happened last night. And in a day or two, whatever mischief Jessica and Lila find on the slopes will upstage you and Todd on Caroline's gossip charts."

Elizabeth rolled her eyes. "Thank goodness for Jessica and Lila."

A pretty, black-haired waitress stopped by to take their breakfast orders and pour coffee. Her name tag read KATHLEEN.

"Excuse me," Enid asked the young woman. "Is there a bookstore or a newsstand within walking distance?"

"Sure," Kathleen replied, her dimples showing

24

when she smiled. "There's a bookstore and gift shop right around the left side of the building. But it's mostly skiing-related stuff—kind of a Colorado theme store." She laughed. "Look for the sign that says ROCKY MOUNTAIN BUY."

"Thanks," Enid said. "I already finished the book I brought to read on the bus, and I'm going to be bored stiff by the time we get to Snow Mountain this evening."

"Snow Mountain, huh?" the waitress asked. "I'm going there myself for a few days—leaving tonight with my husband, as soon as my shift ends. The skiing is supposed to be fantastic this week!"

When the young woman was gone, Elizabeth nodded again toward Lila, Jessica, and Caroline, who had chosen seats at the counter, near the far corner of the diner. "Caroline is sure pumping Jess and Lila for information now," Elizabeth said. "You can see her hanging on every word they say."

"What do you think they're talking about?" Enid asked, her voice surprisingly wistful. Elizabeth looked at her curiously. Enid was gazing at Jessica and Lila with a thoughtful look on her face.

Olivia tore the end of the wrapper off her drinking straw and blew the wrapper at Enid. "What are Jessica and Lila talking about?" she repeated. "Probably one of their usual topics—international

25

politics, maybe. Or neo-Expressionist art. Or world hunger."

Even Enid grinned at that. "More likely," she suggested, "it's a ground-breaking debate on whether black or brown mascara looks better on blondes."

"Nope," Elizabeth said. "You're both wrong. I know my twin. And Jessica's got that gleam in her eyes that she gets for only one subject: *guys.*"

"I think you're right," Olivia decided. "They're both making eyes at that overpumped ski bum at the corner table." She pointed to a handsome, muscular man in his mid-twenties, whose thick white-blond hair looked bleached. "I guess they're getting in some practice for picking up guys on the slopes this week. Notice they made sure to sit within earshot of his table."

"And close enough for him to get a good look at them," said Elizabeth, rolling her eyes. "I, for one, would be happy not to see or be seen by any guys at all for the next week—especially Todd! Do you know that he had the nerve to ask me to eat breakfast alone with him this morning? After what he did last night?"

"Aren't you being pretty hard on him?" Olivia asked carefully. "Maybe you two do need to talk."

"There's nothing to talk about!" Elizabeth insisted. "I can't believe he would embarrass me like that on the bus in the middle of the night—in front of Mr. Collins and everyone!"

"Sure, it was dumb for him to climb into your bunk," Olivia conceded. "But he claims he only wanted to give you a good-night kiss."

"Right," Elizabeth said sarcastically. "In the dark, lying next to me, on a bus full of people. I hate to say it, but maybe Jessica was making sense yesterday."

"This I have to hear," Olivia said. "What did the Psycho Twin say that made sense?"

"She said that Todd is no different from any of those macho types she likes to go out with," Elizabeth replied. "She said that no guy has any real respect for women—that they're all after the same thing."

Enid narrowed her eyes. "That sounds pretty cynical for Jessica."

"No, it wasn't. Not exactly," Elizabeth said, trying to be fair to her sister. "I don't think that's how she meant it. She made romance and love sound like one big, fun game. The object is to have a great time. And to see who wins—the guy or the girl."

"Jessica's wrong, you know," Olivia said. "Sure, some guys are like that. But I think most guys want something more meaningful than that out of a relationship. Don't you think so, Enid?"

Enid shook her head. "I wouldn't know," she

said. "I'm not much of an expert on the subject of relationships lately. But I plan to become an expert."

"What are you talking about?" Elizabeth asked. Enid had a nervous but strangely determined look in her green eyes. "I guess I've been too ticked off at Todd to pay much attention to what's on your mind, Enid. You've been preoccupied all morning. What's wrong?"

"Nothing," Enid said with a nervous giggle. "I'm just coming to some sort of decision, I guess. I'll let you know about it when I've got the details worked out."

She paused for a minute, and Elizabeth was about to press her for more, but Kathleen returned and set their breakfast on the table. As soon as the waitress was gone, Enid spoke up, as if to keep Elizabeth from questioning her further.

"Liz, I think Olivia's right," Enid said. "Some guys are in it for more than cheap thrills."

"Harry and I have a deeper relationship than that," Olivia said, spreading marmalade on an English muffin. She was referring to her boyfriend, Harry Minton, an eighteen-year-old art-school student.

"And you and Todd have a more meaningful relationship than that, too," Enid said. "Lighten up on him, Liz. Listen to what he has to say."

Elizabeth sighed, considering her options as she poured syrup on her French toast. Maybe her friends were right. She always said she trusted Todd. What good was that trust if she wouldn't even listen to his side of the story?

"OK," she agreed finally, spearing a piece of French toast with her fork. "I'll talk to Todd."

Jessica turned around once more to look toward the handsome, muscular skier in the corner. Luckily their classmate Tom McKay had dropped by to talk to Caroline about some skiing lessons he had promised her. Jessica and Lila had taken the opportunity to slip away to the women's room for a confidential chat. Jessica held the door open for Lila and then followed her in.

"Did you check out that guy in the booth in the corner?" Lila asked, pulling out her hairbrush. "You can tell he's a skier from the tan on his face— he's got white goggle marks."

Jessica fished in her purse for a bright red lipstick. "And what a bod!" she exclaimed. She puckered her lips and filled them in with color, scrutinizing herself in the mirror. Jessica knew her jeans were flattering, but she wished she had thought to dress up a little. She sneaked an envious glance in the mirror at Lila's loose silk blouse and leather pants and then looked away quickly, before her friend caught her gaze.

"He must be a weight lifter when he's not skiing," Jessica decided, arranging her bangs with her fingers. "I bet he's got a really cool, masculine name, like Rex."

Lila watched her in the mirror. "I heard Rex saying something to the waitress about how he's going to Snow Mountain," Lila said, challenging Jessica's reflection.

"Yep," Jessica said, returning her glare in the glass. "I heard it, too. And he's mine!"

Lila's lips tightened into a rigid line. "We'll see about that," she said steadily. Her hair crackled with static electricity as she tossed it over her shoulder.

"You think you can have any guy you want just because you're rich!" Jessica said.

"No, I don't," Lila said in a calm, even voice. "I can have any guy I want because I'm rich *and beautiful*."

"Sometimes I can't believe how conceited you are," Jessica began. As usual, she was infuriated—and impressed—by Lila's ability to keep her cool in an argument.

Lila shrugged. "If you've got it, flaunt it."

"Not everything can be *bought*, you know," Jessica said, still glaring at her best friend's smug reflection in the mirror.

"True," said Lila, a thoughtful expression on her face. "At times it makes more sense to lease it for a while."

●　　●　　●

Enid flipped through a book about choosing skis. "No good," she murmured, replacing it on the rack at the Rocky Mountain Buy store. "I've had my skis for years." She glanced at her watch. "But I'd better find something fast," she said under her breath. She'd left Elizabeth and Olivia finishing breakfast in the diner while she went to buy a book. But the bus would be leaving at nine forty-five, and time was running out.

"*Rocks and Minerals of the Rockies*—too boring," she said aloud. "*The History of the Westward Expansion*—too heavy." She sighed and moved on to the fiction rack. She saw romances, mysteries, and historical novels, all set on the ski slopes. But nothing grabbed her attention.

"Rats!" Enid cried, looking at her watch again. She was supposed to be on the bus in five minutes. A table display caught her eye. "*A Hundred and One Ways to Be Sassy on the Slopes,*" Enid read aloud. She picked up a pocket-sized handbook. "What kind of book is that?"

"Actually, it's one of our best-sellers this month," said a gray-haired clerk who was stocking a nearby shelf.

Enid jumped. "Oh, I'm sorry," she said. "I guess I was talking to myself. I didn't see you there."

The woman shrugged. "If you're heading for the slopes, you'll want a copy of this little gem. It's

31

a book of tips for meeting guys on the ski slopes and sweeping them off their feet." She winked. "Our customers say it really works!"

Enid wasn't sure if she should be fascinated or disgusted by the concept. "Romance isn't supposed to be so . . . *planned,*" Enid said. "Is it?"

"Honey, I'll take romance any way I can get it," the woman said. "If I were twenty years younger, I'd be skiing down the intermediate runs at Aspen right now, with a copy of this thing zipped into my snowsuit."

Enid frowned. "I don't know. I'm not usually very aggressive about going after guys."

"Then it seems to me that you need this book even more," the clerk told her. "Besides, even if you're not interested in picking up men, it's entertaining reading."

Enid gazed at the brightly colored cover. "Well, I suppose I could use some entertainment—" she began. A horn blared outside, cutting her off. "Oops," she said. "That's the warning signal. My bus is getting ready to leave."

The older woman smiled. "Try the book, hon," she urged. "I know you won't regret it." Though they were alone in the store, she looked around as if to make sure nobody was listening. "Don't tell my boss," she said, "but if this book doesn't help you meet a handsome skier, you can return it to me on your way home. I'll give you your money back."

Enid smiled. "All right, I'll take it!" she decided. "I can use all the help I can get with those handsome skiers. This is my chance to become a real ski bunny!"

Enid stepped out of the store a few minutes later, feeling absurdly optimistic. Maybe *101 Ways to Be Sassy on the Slopes* was the key to turning her love life around. At the very least it might give her a few ideas.

On the other hand, said a voice in her head, *it seems pitiful that you need a book to tell you how to attract a guy.*

"Oh, well," Enid said aloud, watching her breath turn to ghostly vapor as it hit the cold air. "Not all of us can be naturals at meeting men—like Jessica and Lila."

"You're going to be late," Jessica said to Lila as the bus horn blared outside the diner. Their few remaining classmates ran for the door. But Jessica and Lila still sat side by side at the counter shifting their gazes between each other and the guy they had named Rex.

Lila laughed at Jessica's stubbornness. "That's a ridiculous statement if I ever heard one," she said. "I'm already late. So are you. Not that you've ever cared about being on time for anything in your life."

"I know what you're trying to do," Jessica said. "You're trying to get me to leave the diner first so you can throw yourself at Rex the Bodybuilding Skier when I'm not here to make him fall in love with me instead."

Lila raised her eyebrows. "I don't 'throw myself' at guys," she remarked coolly. "That's your department."

"Well, I don't exactly see Sexy Rexy running over here and begging you to ride the chairlift with him," Jessica pointed out.

"All in good time," Lila said. "Rex is interested. I can tell. He's just waiting for you to leave me alone for a minute so he can come over here to talk to me."

"Ha!" Jessica said. "It's *me* he's waiting to talk to. Admit it, Lila. You saw him looking at me earlier. It's totally obvious who he's interested in."

Lila cocked her head toward Kathleen, the dark-haired waitress. "We'll find out any minute now," Lila said. "The waitress is heading to his table. As soon as she brings Rex his check, I bet he'll waltz right over and ask to borrow my lip balm."

She turned back to Jessica, so as not to appear too eager when the good-looking skier finally made his move. Suddenly Jessica's mouth dropped open. Lila whirled in time to see the waitress lean over to kiss Rex on the forehead. He grasped her hand in a comfortable, familiar manner. And for the first time Lila noticed a wide gold band on his left ring finger—identical to the band on Kathleen's finger.

"What time do you think you'll be home, honey?" Rex asked his wife. "I'd like to set out for Snow Mountain before dark."

"I'm outta here at four," Kathleen responded. "I already packed Joey's stuff, but can you pick up some diapers?"

Lila turned back to Jessica and shook her head. Out of the corner of her eye, she saw Rex's perfect body sauntering out of the diner—to buy disposable diapers.

Lila crossed her arms. "I can't believe you would sit here all this time, Jess, ogling a married man. A man with a baby! Didn't you think to check his ring finger?"

"Me?" Jessica asked, her voice rising an octave. "What about you? Why didn't *you* see his ring? You're the one who's supposed to know about jewelry!"

Lila shook her head. "It's not much of a ring, if you ask me. Twelve-karat gold, tops. Besides, that hand was hidden behind his coffee mug."

"Oh, well," Jessica said with a shrug. "You can't win 'em all." As the bus horn blared again she jumped off her stool and headed toward the door, with Lila following. "So I'll get the next handsome skier instead."

Lila pushed in front of her. "You mean *I'll* get

the next one," she corrected. Lila refused to turn around, but as she shoved the door open she could feel Jessica's eyes burning holes in the back of her expensive new parka.

Elizabeth leaned her cheek against the bus's cold windowpane. Outside, snow drifts were piled four feet high around the parking lot, where the last few Sweet Valley High students were straggling toward the bus. She jumped when the horn blared a second time; her cheekbone banged painfully against the window. She rubbed the side of her face, feeling foolish and a little depressed. She wanted to talk to Todd, to let him apologize for the night before. But she was beginning to feel as if she'd waited too long. She didn't know what to say. "You can apologize now" seemed like a cold way to start a reconciliation.

Enid bounded up the stairs onto the bus, holding a small bag. Under her knit cap, her green eyes were livelier than they'd been in days.

"Enid!" Elizabeth called, patting the bench beside her. "I saved you a seat."

Instead Enid slid into the seat directly behind Elizabeth. "Sorry, Liz," she said, looking toward the back of the bus. "I already promised Olivia I'd sit with her."

Elizabeth stared at her, surprised. It didn't really matter if Enid shared a seat with Olivia. But

36

she distinctly remembered Enid's request for Elizabeth to save her a seat. It wasn't like Enid to forget so quickly. Then she looked up and gulped, suddenly understanding: Todd was heading up the aisle toward her. From the seat behind her, Olivia and Enid both stared at Elizabeth expectantly.

"Uh, Liz?" Todd asked nervously. "Do you mind if I join you?"

Elizabeth wanted to invite him to sit down. But suddenly Mr. Collins's surprised voice sounded in her mind. And the embarrassment of the night before returned, in a hot, uncomfortable blush.

"You didn't bother to ask me before you joined me last night," she said in a low voice.

"I'm sorry about that, Liz," he said. "Really, I am. Please, can we talk about it?"

Elizabeth felt a vague thump from behind her. Olivia was kicking the back of her seat, reminding her that she was supposed to be lightening up on Todd. She looked up into her boyfriend's earnest, handsome face. His brown eyes were full of love—and fear. Suddenly Elizabeth remembered how much she loved him, and the discomfort of the night before faded away.

"Of course we can talk," she decided, flashing him a smile. She felt as though a heavy weight had been removed from her shoulders. "But on one condition," she added. "You have to kiss me first."

37

Chapter 3

The bus lumbered up the mountain road Saturday evening. High overhead, on both sides of the steep canyon, Winston could see tiny skiers gliding down the snowy mountainsides.

Winston gulped. "You didn't tell me the slopes were so steep," he said to Todd, who sat beside him.

Todd shrugged. "What did you expect? It's hard to go downhill skiing without hills."

"Hills?" Winston squeaked. "Those are not hills, Wilkins. Those are the Himalayas!"

"Close," Todd said. "They're the Rockies! There's a one-hundred-eighty-inch base up there. This is going to be awesome!"

"If falling to your death is your idea of a good time."

Todd looked confused. "What's the problem, Winston?" he asked. "You'll do fine."

Winston glanced around carefully to make sure none of the other bus passengers was listening. "Todd, can I tell you a secret?"

"Sure," Todd said with a shrug. "What is it?"

Winston bit his lip. "Do you promise that you won't breathe a word of this to anyone?" he asked.

"Of course," Todd said. "You know I can keep a secret. What's the big deal?"

"Wilkins, I'm a really crummy skier!" Winston revealed, feeling a blush spread across his face.

To Winston's dismay, Todd burst into laughter. "Very funny!" he said. "For a minute there, I thought you were serious."

"I am serious," Winston insisted. "I turn into a complete klutz the moment I strap on a pair of skis. Remember, I'm a southern California boy—sun, surf, and sand. On water skis, I'm unstoppable! On packed powder, I'm hopeless."

"But you've been on plenty of skiing trips before," Todd insisted. "In the snow!"

"Sure I have," Winston admitted. "But how often have you actually seen me on the slopes for more than a few minutes?"

Todd shook his head. "You have a point," he told his friend. "But I could have sworn I heard you saying in the cafeteria the other day that you wanted to ski Devil's Run. That's a double black diamond!"

"A what?" Winston asked.

"An experts-only run," Todd explained. "A regular black diamond run is considered very difficult. A double black diamond is even harder. Devil's Run is the most difficult run on Snow Mountain! Why would you say something like that if you're really a rotten skier?"

Winston shrugged. "A man says a lot of things when athletic types are making a play for his girlfriend."

Todd laughed. "So that's it!" he exclaimed. "And now you have about an hour to figure out how to ski like a pro so nobody will get home next week and tell Maria that you made the whole thing up."

"That's the plan," Winston said. His eyes narrowed when he remembered the way Kirk "the Jerk" Anderson had been eyeing his girlfriend, Maria Santelli, at lunch Thursday. "If I can't become an expert skier in the next few days, there's only one other choice: I break my leg and tell Maria I was caught in an avalanche."

"Egbert," Todd began, "do you ever get tired of getting yourself into these ridiculous situations?"

Winston cocked his head thoughtfully. "No, Todd," he said finally. "I still get a thrill out of it every time."

"Speaking of ways to impress girlfriends," Todd

said, "you do remember our little deal, don't you?"

"I remember," Winston said darkly. "That's the deal where if you and Liz want to be alone in our room, you leave a Do Not Disturb sign on the door, and I quietly slip downstairs to sleep in the lobby. And in return, I get . . ." He stopped. "Just what is it I get out of this deal?"

"My everlasting gratitude," Todd told him.

"Oh, yeah," Winston said. "I knew it was something good. So you—poor guy—will be stuck in our room, making out with a gorgeous blonde. Meanwhile, I will have the pleasure of sleeping on a bumpy couch in a public lobby, feeling the warmth of your gratitude enveloping me."

"Come on, Win," Todd begged. "You know I'd do the same thing for you."

Winston rolled his eyes. "That's easy for you to say. Maria went to Mexico with her parents, remember?"

"Then I'll do you one better," Todd promised.

Winston looked up eagerly. "You'll get me a substitute girlfriend for the week?" he joked.

"Not on your life," Todd said. "But I will give you some skiing tips. Remember, I used to live in Vermont!"

"I'll take all the help I can get," Winston said. "But I don't think it will make much of a difference."

Todd shrugged. "If it doesn't, I promise I'll tell Maria how awesome you were on the slopes. But only if you play along with my Do Not Disturb sign."

"How does Elizabeth feel about this little agreement?" Winston asked.

"Well, she doesn't know about the sign yet," Todd admitted. "But I'm sure she'll love the idea."

"I'm not so sure about that," Winston cautioned. "She was pretty steamed at you about what happened on the bus last night."

"True," Todd said. "But that's because it was in public—and because Mr. Collins caught us. That's why she'll appreciate a private room, where we can really be alone."

"Thanks to me," Winston reminded him. "And see that you remember my selfless sacrifice of a decent night's sleep when—"

He was cut off by the collective cheer that suddenly filled the bus as the Snow Mountain ski lodge came into view. Winston sighed, relieved. Twenty-four hours on a bus was enough for anyone. It would be nice to stand up for a change— even on skis.

"All right!" Todd shouted, clapping Winston on the back a little too hard. Winston grimaced and started stuffing a few belongings into his backpack.

The Swiss-style lodge sat on a snowy rise, a wisp of white smoke trailing into the blue sky from a massive stone chimney. The lodge was backed by steep, skier-dotted ridges on three sides, complete with several chairlifts and an aerial tram with a square red car.

In front of the lodge, just beyond the parking lot where the passengers were stepping off the bus from Sweet Valley, skaters glided over a frozen silver pond. One girl twirled effortlessly in the center, her cherry red scarf fluttering around her like a flag.

Winston stood with the other bus passengers, waiting for his duffel bag to be unloaded. Tall, athletic Claire Middleton gripped his arm and pointed to the highest ridge. "Hey, Winston, I'll race you down the face of Alpine Peak as soon as we've unpacked," she promised.

Mr. Collins cringed. "Please, don't anyone try to be a daredevil right off the bat," he said. "I'd like to see us all get through the week in one piece. I suggest that you start with the easier slopes this evening and work your way up to the more difficult runs."

"No problem, Mr. Collins," Winston said with a heartfelt nod.

"OK, then," Claire said. "I'll race you down one of the gentler slopes for tonight, Win. They've got lighted runs here, so we can still ski for hours!"

"Uh, maybe some other time," Winston said, eyeing the muscular frame of the only girl on Sweet Valley High's varsity football team. "Right now I'm so hungry I could eat a mountain goat."

"Aw, Winston, you're always hungry!" said Jessica, knocking into him with a huge powder blue suitcase. "Hurry up, Lila!" she called, turning around. "We've got to put on our snow-bunny outfits and hit the slopes before all the best-looking skiers have dates for tonight."

"I'm not worried," Lila said. "How much competition can there be?" She cocked her head toward the area behind the bus, where Caroline Pearce seemed to be regaling Olivia Davidson and Patty Gilbert with yet another retelling of the Todd-and-Elizabeth incident from the night before. Winston thought about intervening to set the record straight, but he decided it wasn't necessary. He could hear Olivia sticking up for Elizabeth.

"Besides," Lila continued, still talking to Jessica, "I can't carry all my suitcases by myself. Here comes a porter with a luggage cart."

Winston caught Elizabeth's glance and rolled his eyes. Lila had enough luggage to outfit the Ice Capades. Elizabeth laughed, and Winston was glad he'd drawn her attention away from Caroline's gossip.

As Winston watched, Elizabeth laid a hand on Todd's arm. "So, Todd," she said, "are you up for some skiing right away? Or are you planning to hit the snack bar with Winston first?"

Todd flashed Winston a smile. "Sorry, Win," he said. "But you'll be on your own for dinner." He leaned over and whispered in Winston's ear: "You can't put it off forever, bud. Sooner or later someone's going to see you skiing." Then he turned back to Elizabeth. "I vote for skiing with you," he said eagerly.

Winston and Enid fell into step behind Todd and Elizabeth, and the four began walking toward the lodge.

"Liz?" Enid began hesitantly as Todd held open the door of the lodge. "You and Todd don't mind if I go off skiing on my own, do you?" she asked. "I want to try out a few new moves."

Todd's grin widened. "No problem at all, Enid," he said. "That gives me Liz all to myself."

"Of course we don't mind," Elizabeth said. "But we'll watch for you at the restaurant afterward."

The group passed the huge stone fireplace, which had overstuffed couches drawn up around it. As Winston eyed them warily, Todd swatted him on the shoulder. "Those couches sure look comfortable, don't they, Winston?"

"Yeah," Winston said. "They look great."

The fur lining of her parka hood felt soft and luxurious next to Lila's skin. She inhaled a breath of the cold mountain air and then watched it turn to mist on the wind as she breathed out. Snow Mountain's main chairlift shuddered slightly at some distant impact. One by one, the huge array of lights for night skiing flickered on, illuminating the snow-covered mountainside. On the seat next to Lila, Jessica fidgeted as she scanned the slopes below.

"Calm down, Jessica," Lila admonished her. "It's only a skiing trip. You've been on a dozen of them."

"But never to Colorado!" Jessica said. "Look at all the guys here! Colorado has much better-looking skiers than California does."

Lila shook her head. "I suppose they're all right," she said, remembering the sleek, stylish ski clothes she'd seen on her last trip to Europe with her parents. "But the skiers in the Alps are a lot more sophisticated."

"Well, lah-di-dah!" replied Jessica. "If the guys in this country aren't sophisticated enough for you, then I get dibs on the one in the green-and-white racing suit."

Lila was wearing sunglasses to cut the glare of the lights. Now she raised them and followed Jessica's gaze to a tall, well-built boy of about their age. A fringe of longish hair showed beneath his thick cap.

"Cool goggles," Lila said, noticing his European-style eyewear. "He's probably from Switzerland. But don't get too attached. I think he's with the girl in the tight pink thing."

Jessica frowned. "She's got great taste in guys,

but rotten taste in clothes." She peered up ahead suddenly. "Hey, Li! Check out the dark-haired guy who just jumped off the—" she began, then broke off. "Oops. Forget I mentioned it. It's only Todd, with Liz."

Lila shook her head. "Goody-two-shoes Todd is not exactly my type. But did you see that woman in red giving him the eye?" She pointed to a tall, raven-haired woman of about thirty who was skiing below.

"I wouldn't worry about it," Jessica said with a laugh. "Todd only has eyes for Liz. I swear, those two are so boring—"

"How about that guy over there?" Lila inter-rupted, pointing to a slender blond guy in an Air Force Academy cap. "Some military guys are OK, as long as they're officer material."

"He does have a great body," Jessica agreed. "Look at those shoulders! But I can't tell what his face looks like from here."

"Me neither," Lila said.

"Oh, man!" Jessica exclaimed. "Look at the big, strong-looking sandy-haired guy in the ski patrol uni-form! He looks about twenty-five—too old for a long-term thing, but just right for a spring-break fling!"

Lila shook her head. "Ski patrol guys are all drop-dead gorgeous, but they're no fun. They're too serious about their work to have a good time on the slopes."

47

"Yeah, I guess you're right," Jessica conceded. "All that worrying about safety will do that to you."

"But did you see the two fraternity types who just jumped off the lift, two seats ahead?" Lila asked. "One of them has the best tan I've ever seen, except for on surfers."

"Where did they go?" Jessica asked, her head whipping around. "Rats! I missed them. Wait a minute! We're a lot closer to the ground now, and that Air Force Academy guy is skiing this way. Can you see his face?"

Lila craned her neck to see. Suddenly she realized that she and Jessica were a moment too late to jump easily off the chairlift. "Jess!" she called urgently. She jerked on Jessica's arm and tried to scramble off the edge of the seat. Jessica pulled back until she realized what was happening and then tried to jump without warning, with Lila still tugging on her arm.

To Lila's mortification, both girls slid gracelessly off the chairlift, landing in a snowy heap of tangled poles and skis.

Elizabeth loved the feel of her hair blowing behind her as she glided along a gently sloping trail, away from the crowds. This part of the mountain was utterly silent in the twilight. "This is perfect!"

she called back to Todd. She braked to give him a chance to catch up.

"It sure is," he said, leaning precariously to kiss her on the cheek. "Look! The moon is coming up."

Elizabeth and Todd had skied far enough from the main face of the mountain to be on the very edge of the illuminated slopes. There the sky was dark enough to set off a silver white crescent of moon. The arc had risen just high enough to appear to be balanced between two peaks, which were an inky black against a darkening sky still tinged with pink.

Todd kicked off his skis and reached out to hold Elizabeth from behind. "Now *this* is what I call perfect," he said in a breathless voice, nuzzling the back of her neck.

"Todd!" Elizabeth protested, trying to ignore the warm rush of pleasure she felt at his touch. "That's nice, but it's about the sixth time you've kissed me in the last ten minutes."

Todd shrugged engagingly. "Seven's my lucky number," he said.

Elizabeth smiled. "I know how happy you are that I'm not mad at you anymore," she began. "But this isn't really the time and place for kissing."

"Why not?" Todd asked, gesturing around the snowy ridge. "We're alone here—scout's honor! I guarantee that Mr. Collins will not pop up from behind a snowdrift and order me back to the other side of the mountain."

"That's not the point!" Elizabeth said. "I love it when you kiss me, but I really want to ski tonight. Isn't that why we came up here?"

Todd pointed to her skis and boots. "You *are* skiing!"

"No, I'm not," Elizabeth said. "I'm standing still. And speaking of standing still, it gets awfully cold at nine thousand feet when you're not moving around."

"I'll keep you warm, Liz," Todd promised.

"Later," Elizabeth said pointedly. "Right now let's ski down that trail over there. I remember it from the map—it's called Snowbird Run, and it swings around to bring us back to where everyone else is skiing. I don't even think we're supposed to be on this part of the mountain after dark."

As Todd bent reluctantly to slip his skis back on, Elizabeth pushed off down the trail. A minute later she could hear the swish of his skis behind her as he hurried to catch up. She was glad that he wanted to kiss her, but he really was overdoing it. *He must have been even more upset than he let on about my being mad at him on the bus,* she decided.

"Oh, well," she said under her breath. "He'll get over it and be normal again by tomorrow."

       ❖   ❖   ❖

Jessica tried to look dignified as she disentangled her right arm from around Lila's ski pole. Both girls were sprawled on the hard-packed snow near the end of the chairlift. And one of those huge lights was directly overhead, so every skier on the mountain had probably watched their fall from the lift. Lila was muttering something about its being all Jessica's fault. Jessica ignored her best friend and wiped snow out of her eyes.

As she struggled to her knees, Jessica's mouth dropped open. An incredibly gorgeous guy was standing over her. He was about eighteen years old, with a deep tan, black hair, and brilliant blue eyes. In his red parka and tight black ski pants, he looked like the ultimate ski bum. The sexy skier offered each girl a hand and pulled them to their feet.

"I'm Jessica Wakefield," Jessica blurted out, hoping he would think her face was pink because of the cold.

"I'm Lila Fowler," said Lila at exactly the same instant. Lila laid a hand on the skier's arm in an unnecessary effort to steady herself.

Jessica pretended to lose control of one ski. In her exaggerated attempt to regain her balance, she managed to nudge Lila away from the handsome skier's arm. Then Lila faked a slip, managing to elbow Jessica out of the way. But Lila pushed a little too hard, and both girls ended up sprawled in the snow again.

For a moment Jessica wondered if it was a good idea to pretend to be a klutz. *Maybe I should try to impress him with my expertise on the slopes instead,* she thought. But as soon as the skier opened his mouth, she changed her mind.

"I think you girls could use some lessons," he said, his eyes sparkling with amusement as he helped them up again. Even through his leather gloves, Jessica felt an electric current running from his hand to hers. "My name is Lucas King, and I'm a ski instructor here," he said with a smile.

Jessica grinned back. "A ski instructor?" she asked innocently, sneaking a glance at Lila.

"How lucky that we ran into you," Lila said, brushing snow off her pants. "Do you have any tips for us?"

"Sure," Lucas said, his blue eyes twinkling. "Here's your first lesson, and it's absolutely free. Try taking the other chairlift next time. Most of the slopes on this ridge of the mountain are marked as blue runs—that means they're for intermediate skiers. From the looks of things, you two will want to try the green runs—the beginner slopes. Take the little chairlift just behind the lodge. It leads to the bunny trails."

"Bunny trails, huh?" Jessica asked. "Just the

place for a couple of snow bunnies like us!"

Lucas laughed. "Something like that," he said, pulling his goggles down over his eyes. "Well, if you want any further lessons, just ask for me around the lodge," he called over his shoulder. A red bandanna fluttered behind him as he skied away.

"You can close your mouth now," Lila said as soon as he was gone.

"Close your own mouth," Jessica replied. Her eyes were still riveted on Lucas's tall, lean body as he glided gracefully down the slope. "You know, I thought I was a great skier. But I've just decided that I could use some private tutoring from an expert."

"Good," Lila said. "I hear Enid's a real pro. She can give you some pointers while I'm having my private lesson with Lucas King."

Jessica's eyes narrowed. Lila was used to getting her way in everything just because she was filthy rich. Well, this was one time when Jessica was going to win. "Don't even think about it," she warned. "I saw him first."

"Come off it, Jess," Lila said. "We saw him at exactly the same time. But he only helped you up to be polite. Anybody could see that I was the one he couldn't take his eyes off."

"Only because you looked so silly with all that snow on your face," Jessica retorted. "He'd probably never seen a sixteen-year-old girl with a white beard."

"Sorry, Jess. But Lucas is going to make his choice—and you're going to be left out in the cold."

"Oh, he'll make his choice, all right," Jessica agreed. "And you're the one who will be left riding solo on the chairlift—that is, if you can manage it without falling off."

Lila put her hands on her hips. "Is that so?" she asked, her eyes colder than the snow that had found its way up Jessica's sleeve in their last fall. That look in Lila's eyes was usually enough to make any opponent back down. But Jessica wasn't just any opponent. And she didn't plan to let Lila intimidate her into giving up Lucas without a fight. "How about putting your money where your mouth is?" Lila asked. "If you're so sure that Lucas likes you better, then you won't object to a little wager."

"No way, Lila!" Jessica protested. "Everything's about money with you, isn't it? You're well aware that this trip has cleaned out every cent I've got. Money is the one area where I can't compete with you, and you know it."

Lila straightened her parka. "One of many," she said pointedly. She sighed as Jessica glared at her. "Oh, all right," Lila said finally. "What about a different kind of deal? I bet you that I will kiss Lucas King—on the lips—before you do. And when I do, you have to ski Devil's Run!"

"Devil's Run?" Jessica asked, feeling her face pale. "Lila, that's way up at the top of Alpine Peak. It's the most dangerous run on the mountain. Sure, we're good skiers. But we're not Olympic athletes! We can't handle a double black diamond run!"

Lila folded her arms in front of her. "I'm not afraid of Devil's Run," she said. "On the other hand, *my* fear isn't what matters, since I plan to win this bet. But I don't blame you for being so sure that you'll lose. If you're scared, I'm sure Lucas—"

"Wait a minute!" Jessica interrupted. "I didn't say I was scared. And I'm not going to lose. I was just worried that *you* weren't up to skiing Devil's Run—after *I* kiss Lucas first."

"Does that mean we have a bet?" Lila asked. "Should we set some ground rules?"

"We have a bet, all right," Jessica replied. "And it has to be a secret, so that neither of us can get— or *buy*—any help. We don't tell any of our friends."

"Or sisters," Lila added pointedly.

"Or sisters," Jessica agreed, inwardly cursing Lila's thoroughness. "Besides that, there are no rules. All's fair in love and war—and I do mean *war*. Anything goes in the Battle of Snow Mountain. Absolutely anything."

Lila smiled. "You're on," she said.

◦　　◦　　◦

Enid held one glove in her teeth while she struggled with the ornery zipper on the pocket of her old green parka. She had read most of her new book on the bus, but now she was determined to start at the beginning and try every single one of the 101 ways to be sassy on the slopes. She yanked out the book and reread the first tip.

"'Method One,'" she read aloud. "'You have to protect your face from sunburn and windburn, anyway. So why not do it in a way that attracts attention from skiers of the opposite sex? Fluorescent-colored zinc oxide gets you noticed. Most ski shops will carry your usual SPF number in a variety of fashion colors—or pick a hue that coordinates with your ski clothes. For a little extra attention, try wearing zinc oxide—in your favorite glow-in-the-dark shade—while night skiing. Guys love a girl who isn't afraid to look a little bit wild.'"

"Here's to taking a walk on the wild side," Enid said, pulling out the fluorescent lime green sunblock stick she'd bought at the lodge's ski shop. "The book's right. It's all about getting noticed."

She took a deep breath and smeared the green sunblock on her nose, surprised at her own courage. Then she stuffed the book and the sunblock back into her parka pocket, replaced her glove, and skied slowly toward the chairlift with what she hoped was a daring smile on her face.

To Enid's surprise, the fluorescent color attracted a guy right off the bat.

"Awesome nose color, dude!" came the nasal voice of the boy next to her in the lift line. He was wearing baggy black jeans and a black-and-gray plaid flannel shirt that was big enough for an entire bobsled crew.

The book hadn't said so, but Enid was positive that sassy ski bunnies were open-minded about men. She tried to tell herself that she shouldn't be put off by little things like nose rings, Technicolor hair, and shirts that hadn't been washed since leap year.

"Your nose, like, matches my hair!" the boy continued, a look of awe on his face. He was nodding as if his head were on a spring.

Enid raised her eyebrows. "But isn't your hair, uh, purple?" she asked.

The boy flicked back a long violet lock that had fallen over his forehead. "That's only, like, in the front," he informed her. "To match my socks. But in the back, man, my hair is like, totally green." He turned his head, and sure enough, a lime green ponytail straggled down the back of his shirt.

"Yeah, that's the same shade as my sunblock, all right," Enid said through clenched teeth.

"You got some style, babe," the boy continued. "I like chicks with style. Wanna ride the lift with me? I'll show you my socks."

"Uh, maybe some other time," Enid said. "I, um, just realized that I forgot my—my nose ring. I'll go back to my room to get it. Maybe I'll catch up with you later."

Enid skied away as though she were competing for a spot on the Olympic ski team. As soon as she was out of sight of the chairlift, she used the back of her glove to wipe the lime green sunblock from her nose.

Sighing, she took Method One off her mental list. Maybe Method Two would attract a different class of ski bum. She hoped it would at least attract someone from her own solar system.

Being sassy was turning out to be a lot harder than it looked.

A half hour later Todd stood at the bottom of the main chairlift, waiting for Elizabeth to join him in line for their final run of the evening. He easily picked her out on the broad, flat saddle at the bottom of the slope, wedeling gracefully toward him in her navy ski pants and parka. She was still a few minutes away.

As usual, he couldn't help thinking that Elizabeth was just about the prettiest, sexiest girl in the world. He wished she had been a little more receptive to his kisses earlier. But maybe she was still shy about public displays of affection since the incident on the bus Friday night. Todd knew he'd really blown it, allowing Mr. Collins to catch them like that. As soon as he and Elizabeth were truly alone, he was sure she would be as warm and loving as he could want. He grinned, thinking of his room at the lodge and the DO NOT DISTURB sign.

Suddenly a woman in a clingy red one-piece ski suit skidded to a dramatic, curving stop nearby, spraying him with an arc of snow. Todd blinked.

"Need a lift partner?" she asked in a low, throaty voice.

Todd couldn't help feeling flattered. She was much older—thirty or so—but sexy, with curly black hair and a lot of curves. But Elizabeth was on her way down the slope, and he was in love with Elizabeth.

"Uh, no, thanks," he said, shaking his head. "I'm waiting for someone."

The woman followed his gaze to Elizabeth's trim, navy-suited form in the distance. "Don't wait too long," the older woman warned. "Standing in the cold will give you frostbite."

Todd watched as she skied away. Something about the woman was extremely unnerving.

Chapter 4

"Let's do one more run," Lila suggested as she and Jessica stepped into the short line of skiers waiting for the chairlift. "Then we should get back to the lodge for dinner."

Jessica gritted her teeth at Lila's bossy tone. Lila was always so quick to make decisions for everyone around her. Sometimes it drove Jessica crazy. But her mind was racing, working on a plan for stealing Lucas away from Lila. For now, it was safer to let Lila think she had Jessica cowed.

"Sure, Lila," Jessica said in an agreeable tone. She pretended to be glancing around casually as she waited for the lift. In reality, she was scanning the crowd for a glimpse of Lucas King's red parka.

"Come on, Jess," Lila said sharply. "We're up next for the chairlift."

The swinging chair moved toward the girls. Suddenly Jessica spotted a flash of red as Lucas skied by. Lila flexed her knees to let the lift scoop her up. But Jessica ducked and whirled around, nearly banging her head on the moving chair. Then she was off down the slope, racing after Lucas. Lila, alone on the lift seat, angrily waved a pole at her.

From her seat on the chairlift, Enid watched as a great-looking guy in a red parka flew down the mountain below her. She sneaked a glance at the middle-aged woman who sat beside her on the lift. The woman's face was partly hidden by a purple hat, but she seemed entranced by the carnival of brightly dressed skiers flowing down the mountainside. She wasn't likely to pay much attention if her seatmate pulled out a book.

The zipper on Enid's parka pocket stuck for a moment, but Enid managed to wrench it open. She slipped out the small book, feeling almost as if she were doing something illegal. She had decided not to tell her friends about her game plan for now. It was too embarrassing to need a book in order to pick up guys—especially if the only guys who were going to show any interest turned out to be like the Green Ponytail Dude.

Elizabeth would certainly be sympathetic. But Elizabeth would never be able to relate to Enid's problem. With her wholesome good looks and ease with people, Elizabeth Wakefield could have any guy she wanted—if she hadn't been a hundred percent loyal to Todd. Enid loved Elizabeth like a sister, but she couldn't help being a teensy bit envious of her best friend's beauty and popularity. Maybe *101 Ways to Be Sassy on the Slopes* could help Enid learn some of the secrets that came so naturally to girls like Elizabeth.

Enid opened the book to the second technique.

"'Method Two,'" she read under her breath. "'Dare to be skillful.'"

"Did you say something?" asked the woman in the purple hat.

"Uh, no," Enid replied. "Nothing at all." The woman turned away, and Enid went back to her book, reading silently this time.

Contrary to popular belief, the author continued, *acting helpless is not always the best way to attract a man. Being a woman is fully compatible with being strong, capable, and athletic. If you're a terrific skier, flaunt your skill; don't hide it. When you see a guy who could use some help on the slopes, give him a few tactful pointers. He'll love you for it.*

Enid nodded slowly. Unlike the lime green sunscreen, Method Two was good advice. In fact, it was the kind of advice Elizabeth would have given her.

Enid knew she was a terrific skier. She'd honed her skills on frequent trips to her aunt Nancy's cabin near Lake Tahoe. But did she have the nerve to ski up to a complete stranger on the slopes and offer him some tips on the correct form for snowplowing?

She sighed, afraid that she knew the answer. After her first experience with sassiness on the slopes, Enid was reluctant to chance a second encounter with alien life forms. *Maybe for the rest of tonight,* she thought, *I'll just scope out the possibilities and get the lay of the land.*

She would dare to be skillful the next day.

The seat rocked as Lila waved her pole at Jessica's retreating back. "Jessica, you little creep!" Lila yelled, noticing the red blur of Lucas's parka and bandanna. "How dare you!" she cried. Then she felt an uncharacteristic blush spreading over her face. Losing her cool was not Lila's style. People were looking.

Lila took a deep breath and tried to appear dignified. Jessica might think she'd won this round. But Jessica was wrong. Nobody made a fool out of Lila Fowler. Nobody.

"I'll get Jessica for this," Lila vowed. She wondered if she could buy one of those Saint Bernard dogs that hung out around ski slopes in old movies, wearing barrels around their necks—one that was trained to *eat* manipulative blond ski bunnies.

For a moment Lila remembered herself and Jessica in the Caribbean, fighting over Mick Myers, a gorgeous windsurfing instructor. The episode was an embarrassing one; eventually they'd learned that the sleazebag was secretly dating both of them, as well as several other girls. The trip had ended with Jessica and Lila working together on a brilliant scheme to humiliate Mick in front of everyone—and realizing that their friendship was more important than any guy.

Lila pressed her lips together into a hard, straight line. At the moment she wasn't so sure about her friendship with Jessica. Of course, she couldn't be completely sure of Lucas, either. He seemed like a genuinely nice person, but Lila would be careful. She wasn't about to let another cute guy use her. On the other hand, if getting close to Lucas would take Jessica's ski cap down a few sizes—well, that was exactly what she would do.

Lila would have Lucas for herself. And she would watch Jessica fall flat on her face as she slid down Devil's Run.

This was war.

Jessica skied a gently sloping tier of the mountainside, heading toward Lucas. "Where's your friend?" he asked, looking up from unfastening his skis. At the last minute Jessica remembered that she was supposed to be a crummy skier, and she made a point of stumbling a little.

"Steady, Jessica!" Lucas said, catching her shoulders in his hands as she skidded to a shaky stop.

Jessica ignored the fact that he had asked about Lila before he'd even said hello. "Thanks, Lucas," she said, startled and entranced by the intense blue of his eyes. "I don't know what I would have done without you."

"I'm surprised to see you without your friend," Lucas began. "Uh, what was her name? I thought you two pretty much had to hang on to each other for dear life to keep yourselves from tumbling to the foot of the mountain."

Jessica grinned. He didn't even remember Lila's name. *Score one for the Wakefield twin.*

"Oh, Lila went back to the lodge," Jessica said. "She decided she wasn't cut out to be a skier." She sighed and batted her eyelashes. "So I'll just have to find someone else to hang on to for dear life."

She placed her hand on Lucas's shoulder for balance as she struggled with the bindings on one ski.

"Here, let me show you," he said, unfastening her boot for her. "You really are a novice at this, aren't you?"

Jessica shrugged. "I'm sure I could learn," she said. "I mean, if I had the right teacher."

"So you want to take me up on my offer to give you some lessons?" Lucas asked. Snow flurries were just beginning to fall, and Jessica longed to reach up and brush them from his thick black hair.

"Definitely!" she said.

"Will an hour do it?" Lucas asked. "Or should I sign you up for two?"

"Oh, no!" Jessica said quickly, shaking her head so that her hair caught the light. She hoped the glittering snowflakes looked as sexy in her hair as they did in his. "This is something I'm really serious about getting good at," Jessica continued. "I think a whole day of private tutoring would just about do it."

Lucas seemed surprised and pleased. "A whole day?" he asked. "Jessica, are you sure you can afford that? A day of private lessons can run into some serious money."

"Don't worry about that," Jessica assured him. "My parents gave me their credit card for the week. And they told me to have a good time." In reality, the credit card was for emergencies, and they had given it not to Jessica but to her more responsible twin, Elizabeth. And the encouragement about having a good time had been part of an entirely separate conversation. But Lucas didn't have to know that.

Besides, Jessica thought, *this is an emergency.*

She had to keep Lucas away from Lila. And she had to impress him with how much her skiing would improve in just one day.

Lucas looked at her thoughtfully. "All right, Jessica," he said finally. "I think it's great how determined you are to become a better skier. I already have a few students lined up for tomorrow, but I'll go to the lodge now and reassign them to one of the other instructors. You've got yourself an all-day tutor."

Jessica wanted to jump up and down in the snow. Instead she smiled her sexiest smile and thanked him.

"Let's go out early and plan to stick with the lower slopes," Lucas said thoughtfully, scanning the sky as though he could read it in the dark. "The ski patrol says a bad storm may be headed for the higher elevations late tomorrow afternoon."

"That makes a lot of sense," Jessica said seriously. "I wouldn't want to get in over my head."

He saluted with one finger and turned to go. Jessica felt her knees melting at the sexy, European-looking gesture. Then she stood admiring Lucas's tight black ski pants as he walked off carrying his skis.

Jessica hoisted her own skis over her shoulder and sauntered toward the restaurant. She felt a twinge of guilt over running up such a huge bill on her parents' credit card for skiing lessons. But she brushed it aside. After all, that was what her parents' credit card was for.

After a late dinner Saturday night, Elizabeth and Todd lounged by the stone fireplace at the lodge, letting the heat soak into their limbs.

Elizabeth shifted her body on the overstuffed upholstery, already feeling a slight soreness in her legs from the unaccustomed exercise. "Have you heard of this new kind of ski goggles?" she asked Todd, holding up the magazine she was reading. "Some special coating on the lenses really cuts down on the glare. Maybe I should try a pair."

Todd took the magazine from her as if he was interested in ski goggles. But he yawned deeply, closed the magazine, and laid it on the table. "Maybe we should head upstairs," he said slowly.

Elizabeth caught his yawn and returned it. "Good idea," she said. "It's a little early, but I'm tired, too. We should get a good night's sleep so we can be fresh in the morning for a whole day on the slopes. But where's Winston? I haven't seen him since dinner."

Todd shrugged and helped her to her feet. "I think he was going to see what the indoor pool looks like," he said as they walked toward the elevator arm in arm. "Winston says he plans to spend a lot of the week in the hot tub."

"That doesn't sound like Winston," Elizabeth said. "I'd have expected to see him hotdogging all over the mountain. I was surprised he didn't go skiing tonight."

Todd laughed and then changed the subject. "What about Enid?" he asked. "She seemed quiet at dinner."

"I'm not sure," Elizabeth said. "Something was bothering her on the trip here. She seems to have worked it out, but she hasn't told me about it yet. I think she will soon, though. I don't want to press her too hard."

They stepped off the elevator at the fifth floor, and Elizabeth turned toward her room, which was in the wing opposite Todd and Winston's.

"Wait a minute!" Todd said suddenly. "Don't you want to see where I'm staying?"

Elizabeth raised her eyebrows. "Why? Isn't it just like my room?" she asked. "I mean, both rooms are on the same floor of the same lodge. How unique can yours be?"

"Aw, come on," Todd pleaded, "just for a minute." He smiled winsomely, and Elizabeth felt her logic melting. Todd probably just wanted a little privacy for a good-night kiss. She wouldn't have minded kissing him in the hallway, but it was sweet of him to be so concerned about her reputation, especially after the incident on the bus.

"OK," Elizabeth agreed. "Let's go see your room."

Jessica guessed that it was after nine o'clock on Saturday night when she finally settled into a back booth at the hotel restaurant to get some dinner. She was ravenous, but she was also pleased with herself. She'd managed to schedule a whole day alone with Lucas—and she'd done it right under Lila's snobby, upturned little nose. Jessica grinned and sipped a hot chocolate while she waited for her friend.

"Hey, Lila!" she called heartily as Lila stomped into the room. Lila still held her skis over her shoulder; her face was practically purple with rage under the rabbit-fur-lined hood. "How was your last run?" Jessica asked sweetly as Lila approached the table.

"Speaking of runs," Lila fumed, "if you do an end run around me again, Jessica Wakefield, I swear I'll make you sorry!"

"Whatever do you mean?" Jessica asked innocently. She smiled when she saw that the two fraternity brothers from the chairlift were sitting at the next table, listening with obvious amusement.

Lila noticed, too. She took a deep breath and

slid into the seat across from Jessica, leaning her skis against the edge of the table.

"You know exactly what I mean," Lila replied in a low voice. "I just went to the lodge to book a lesson with Lucas for the morning."

Jessica took another sip of her hot chocolate. "Oh, really?" she asked. "You've got to try these fried cheese sticks, Lila," she added. "I thought we could use an appetizer before we order dinner."

"Don't change the subject!" Lila said. But she accepted a cheese stick and wrenched off the end of it with her teeth, reminding Jessica of a bulldog wrestling with a bone. A very expensive, pedigreed bulldog.

Jessica shrugged. "So, did you book your ski lesson with Mr. King?" she asked.

"I couldn't," Lila informed her. "But then you already knew that. It seems that Lucas's dance card is filled for tomorrow. A certain Ms. J. Wakefield has scheduled an all-day lesson."

"Oh, that's right," Jessica said. "I forgot all about that. I thought a whole day of intense work, one on one, would be just the ticket to improve my skiing. I've always wanted to build up my speed, you know."

"You're already the *fastest* girl around," Lila said acidly. "But you're crazy if you think you're going to get Lucas all to yourself tomorrow.

71

We're sharing that all-day lesson. Period."

Jessica shrugged, trying to appear nonchalant. "I told you that all's fair in love and war," she reminded Lila. "It looks to me as if the Battle of Snow Mountain has begun, and you just lost a round."

Lila's face looked as if it were carved out of ice.

Suddenly a marvelously simple plan materialized in Jessica's mind. "Oh, all right," she agreed, trying to sound reluctant. "Have it your way. Lucas and I are meeting at the bunny hill tomorrow morning at nine o'clock," she added. "You're welcome to come along."

"I hope you realize now that you can't get the best of me," Lila said. "Your tricks are too transparent."

Jessica sighed. "I know, I know. But it doesn't matter. Even with both of us there, Lucas will like me best. You just wait and see."

Todd swung open the paneled door of his room at the lodge and ushered Elizabeth in. He watched her lithe figure as she walked around the room, glancing at the rustic wood furniture and the snow-scene prints on the walls.

"It really does look exactly like my room," Elizabeth said. With her toe, she nudged a pair of sneakers that lay in the center of the floor. "Except that Enid and I don't have Winston's

72

size-thirteen high-tops decorating our carpet."

She walked to the window and lifted the heavy white curtain as Todd reached around the door to slip the DO NOT DISTURB sign over the knob. Then he turned back toward Elizabeth and admired the gentle curve of her cheek, which glowed softly in the reflected light from the slopes outside.

"Your view is a little different from mine and Enid's," Elizabeth said as he walked up behind her. "You're facing the west slopes, and we're facing Alpine Peak and the other tall ridges to the east."

"I like the view from here just fine," Todd said.

"It is really nice," Elizabeth agreed, letting the curtain drop. "But I'm pooped. I think it's time to get back to my own room and put on my flannel pajamas."

She started for the door, but Todd waylaid her in the middle of the room. He slipped his arms around her and marveled, as he always did, about how neatly their bodies seemed to fit together. He pressed his lips against hers and felt a roar of heat through his limbs as her lips parted slightly and softened against his.

At last, Todd thought, *everything is perfect*. Winston would see the sign on the doorknob and stay away. And Todd and Elizabeth could sleep in each other's arms. Todd slowly sat on the bed, pulling Elizabeth along with him. She was murmuring something into his ear, and he was mesmerized by the whisper of her breath against the tender skin on the side of his neck.

Then he made out her words: "Todd, cool it!" she ordered.

"We don't have to be cool anymore, Liz," he said, nibbling at her neck. "We're alone now."

"I don't know what's gotten into you lately!" she complained.

"Nothing's gotten into me," Todd said, lowering his voice as he gently kissed her left ear. "I just want to remind you of how much I love you."

"I love you, too," Elizabeth said. "But I don't think this is such a good idea."

"You don't have to worry about Winston barging in on us," Todd assured her. "I arranged for him to sleep somewhere else tonight. We have this room to ourselves for as long as we want it."

"You arranged for Winston to—" Elizabeth stopped, flustered. Then she extracted herself from Todd's grasp and stepped quickly toward the bathroom. "Hold on a minute," she called over her shoulder. Todd smiled. Now that Elizabeth knew they had real privacy, she just wanted to freshen up a little before getting more intimate. He heard the gurgle of water running in the sink as he plumped up the pillows and sat back against them. A moment later he smiled lazily as Elizabeth walked toward him, holding a glass of water in her hand.

"Now where did we leave off?" Todd asked, reaching out for her.

"Right about here," she said. She pressed her lips together and dumped the glass of water in his lap.

Todd gasped as the cold water splashed against his jeans. Elizabeth wheeled on her heel and left the room.

As the door slammed behind her, Todd could have sworn that a cold wind howled through the room. He sighed and fell back on the bed, feeling utterly defeated.

Chapter 5

Jessica stepped out of the bathroom wearing her pink terry-cloth robe and a pair of thick, warm socks. "I'm finished brushing my teeth," she said to Lila, whose face was covered with a bright blue facial mask. "The bathroom is all yours, Li—even if you do look like the Creature from the Blue Lagoon."

"Just a second, Jess," Lila responded. She reached for the telephone receiver and keyed in a number as she spoke to her roommate. "You did say our lesson is at nine o'clock in the morning, didn't you?" she asked Jessica.

Jessica pulled a bottle of lemon-scented nail polish remover from her make-up bag. "That's right," she said.

"Hello, is this the front desk?" Lila asked into

the phone, carefully holding the receiver away from her slick blue face. "This is Lila Fowler in room five-eighteen. I need a wake-up call for seven forty-five tomorrow morning. . . . Thank you."

Like twin otters peering out through holes in a frozen lake, Lila's brown eyes stared triumphantly through her ice blue mask. "I'm glad you finally decided to act like an adult about this thing with Lucas," she said, a little too politely. She still sounded suspicious, as if she didn't quite believe that Jessica didn't have another trick up her sleeve.

"Oh, well," Jessica said. "I figure that no matter what we do, in the end Lucas will have to make up his own mind."

"True," Lila agreed.

"I still think he'll pick me, of course," Jessica continued. "But if he doesn't, well, there's not much I can do about it. Anyway, I'm finished in the bathroom, if you need to wash that blue gunk off your face."

Lila glanced at her speculatively, as if trying to read her mind. "What are you going to be doing while I'm in there?" she asked suspiciously.

Jessica shrugged. "Nail polish," she said, holding up a bottle.

"I suppose you can't get into much trouble if you don't have the use of your hands," Lila said grudgingly.

"Trouble?" Jessica asked. "Me? I hardly know the definition of the word."

"Jessica, right under *trouble* in the dictionary, there's a little picture of you," Lila retorted. She stood in the open doorway of the bathroom. "Just try to stay out of it for the next ten minutes, OK?"

"Stay out of trouble?" Jessica asked, unscrewing the cap of the nail polish bottle. "Or out of the dictionary?"

"You? Looking in a dictionary?" Lila retorted. "Not much danger of that!" The bathroom door swung shut behind her.

For a moment Jessica remained on the bed, nail polish poised in her hand. Then she heard the whoosh of water running in the sink and sprang into action. She tiptoed to the door and stepped into the hallway.

Elizabeth paced from one end of the room to the other. She couldn't believe that Todd would have the nerve to ask her to stay in his room all night. She opened her mouth to complain to Enid but closed it again. Enid was absorbed in a pocket-sized book that she'd picked up at the rest stop that morning. Already in her nightgown, Elizabeth's roommate was sitting on the chair by the window with her legs tucked up under her as her green eyes moved across the pages.

Elizabeth sighed and pulled a pair of pajamas from a dresser drawer. She might as well get ready for bed, too. She jumped, startled, when someone knocked at the door.

"Go to bed, Todd!" Elizabeth called. "I really don't want to talk about it right now."

Enid looked up, concern etched on her round, pretty face.

Elizabeth gave her a wan smile. "It's OK," she said. "I'll tell you all about it later."

"Lizzie!" came a stage whisper from outside the door. "It's not Todd! It's me, Jess!"

Elizabeth swung open the door to find her sister standing outside, bouncing impatiently in her socks. She wore a pink bathrobe that was exactly like the blue one that hung on the hook on Elizabeth's side of the closet.

"Come in," Elizabeth told her. "I wasn't expecting to see you here tonight—especially in your bathrobe."

"I can only stay a second," Jessica blurted. "I'm in a rush. Liz, can you give me a wake-up call in the morning? I don't trust the front desk to get it right!"

Elizabeth shook her head. "What's going on, Jessica? Since when do you care what time you get up?"

"Since I finagled a hot date with a ski instructor,"

Jessica explained hurriedly. "Please, Lizzie! I don't have much time!"

"Sure," Elizabeth said with a shrug. "What time do you need me to wake you up?"

"What time are you getting up?" Jessica asked, glancing down the hall toward her own room, a few doors away and across the hall.

"Seven o'clock," Elizabeth said.

"Great!" Jessica replied. "As soon as you're awake, run down to my room and tap on the door. It's number five-eighteen. But be careful not to wake Lila! She wants to sleep late."

Jessica scurried back to her own room, a blur of pink. Elizabeth shook her head and shut the door behind her.

"What was that all about?" Enid asked.

"With Jessica," said Elizabeth, "it's usually safer not to know."

At seven thirty on Sunday morning a shadowy figure eased open the door of Todd's room and crept inside. With the shades drawn, the room was as dark as midnight. Slowly the lanky figure tiptoed across the floor, listening to the slow, steady breathing that emanated from the mass of darker dimness that was Todd's bed.

Suddenly the intruder stumbled on something—a pair of shoes left in the middle of the rug.

He swore, and the light by the bed switched on.

"Winston!" Todd said in a sleepy voice as he squinted at his roommate. He sat up in bed. "What the heck—"

Winston used his hand to shield his eyes from the bed. "Sorry, Todd. Sorry, Liz," he said in a rush. "I didn't mean to—"

"It's all right, Winston," Todd assured him. "Elizabeth isn't here."

Winston heaved a huge sigh of relief and plopped himself down on the foot of Todd's bed. "Whew!" he said. "Am I glad you're alone! I have never been so embarrassed in all my life."

Todd shrugged. "Practice makes perfect."

"Sorry to sneak in like that," Winston said. "But I was downstairs on one of those darn uncomfortable couches, which, by the way, were designed for munchkins, and the morning desk clerk was giving me the evil eye. I was afraid he'd have me arrested if I didn't get out of there."

"Well, it's your room, too," Todd said obligingly.

"Only when you and Liz aren't in here having some, uh, quality time," Winston said. "Man, was I glad to hear you say she's already gone back to her own room!"

"Winston, she left almost ten hours ago," Todd informed him. "I couldn't get her to stay last night."

"No!" Winston said, shaking his head. "I didn't hear you right. I thought you just said that you were here alone all night in this room—this room that is half mine. But that couldn't be what you really said. I mean, the Do Not Disturb sign was out, so I naturally assumed—"

"Sorry," Todd said. "I guess I forgot to take in the sign after Elizabeth threw water on my, um, plans for the evening."

"Do you mean to tell me that I spent a whole night sleeping on a short, squashy munchkin couch, roasting myself in front of that kiln they call a fireplace, for no reason at all?"

Todd nodded. "Yep, that's about the size of it."

"Why didn't you come downstairs and get me?"

"I was upset about Elizabeth's leaving," Todd admitted. "I guess my head wasn't on straight."

"It's going to be a lot more crooked when I get finished with it!" Winston threatened, rising to his feet. He took in Todd's broad shoulders and basketball-conditioned body and compared them to his own skinny form. Then he slumped back onto the bed. "But maybe I'll get a few hours of sleep first."

"You planning on doing any skiing today?" Todd asked halfheartedly.

Winston shrugged. "I might as well," he said. "My muscles are already writhing in pain from sleeping on that stupid little couch. If I'm going to spend the rest of my life in traction, I might as well have an impressive excuse to give Maria."

Jessica grabbed Lucas's arm when the seat on the chairlift rocked suddenly. "I can't believe I'm actually going to be skiing from so high up!" she marveled.

"I can't believe you're already off the bunny slopes," Lucas said, his eyes even bluer than the brilliant morning sky. "It's only nine thirty in the morning, and after a day of stumbling around on your own, and an hour of lessons this morning, you're heading to the easiest of the blue runs. I've never seen anyone who was such a natural."

Jessica smiled. "It's only because I have such a great teacher," she said modestly. "But Lucas, those peaks look pretty steep. Do you think I'm ready for them?"

"Jessica, from what I've seen, I'd say you could manage anything you set your mind to."

Including a kiss? Jessica wondered, eyeing his perfect profile and full, sensuous lips. "Just how hard is Devil's Run?" she asked suddenly, thinking of Lila.

"Devil's Run?" Lucas asked, his eyes wide. "I swear, I've never met anyone who could surprise me the way you do. Devil's Run is really tough,

Jess. And dangerous. A lot of expert skiers wipe out on the double black diamonds. I suggest you stick to the blue runs for now."

"Oh," Jessica said, feeling a pang of remorse about the possibility of sending Lila down such a treacherous run. *But it's Lila's own fault,* said a voice inside Jessica's head. *This whole bet was her idea, not mine.*

"Don't be too disappointed," Lucas said, giving her hand a squeeze. "You're doing great, even if you're not ready for Devil's Run. By the end of the week, I bet everyone will think you've been skiing for years!"

Lila sat up in bed. She stretched luxuriously against the clean cotton sheets. They weren't satin, like at home, but they would do. She'd slept marvelously well. In fact, she was amazed that her eyes were open even before her seven forty-five wake-up call.

She grabbed the spare pillow from her bed and prepared to throw it at Jessica as a special kind of wake-up call. But she stopped, surprised. Jessica's unmade bed was empty. The bathroom door was open, and Lila couldn't hear water running in the shower or sink.

She glanced at the clock and her eyes widened. She jumped out of bed, grabbed the telephone, and called the front desk. "It's ten thirty in the morning!" Lila screeched at the stuttering clerk. "I specifically requested a wake-up call for seven forty-five, for a very important meeting this morning. Can't you people get anything right?"

"I-I'm sorry, Ms. Fowler," the baffled man stammered through the phone. "But our records show that you phoned us back a few minutes later and canceled that wake-up call."

Lila slammed down the phone. She hadn't phoned the desk to cancel her wake-up call, but she had a good idea who had.

"Jessica!" she screamed, punching the feather pillow. "This time you've gone too far!"

Enid jumped off the tram car around noon on Sunday. "Method Two is my ticket to romance," she said in a determined voice. "Today I'm going to be sassy on the slopes if it kills me."

She pushed off with her poles and slalomed along a moderately difficult run, relishing the feel of the wind against her face. The snow was a lot deeper than the day before. The previous night's snowstorm must have gotten worse after she went to bed. In fact, Enid had noticed a sign posted near the ski patrol station at the tram depot on the summit, warning skiers of potential avalanche conditions on some of the high eastern slopes. She wasn't worried. She was skiing west.

She began scanning the nearby skiers to see if any guys looked as if they could use a few pointers from an expert woman like herself—a woman who dared to be a skillful skier.

After a few minutes she discovered her mistake. "Guys who are crummy skiers are on the easier runs," she realized aloud. "How stupid of me!" Being sassy on the slopes took a lot more planning than she'd thought.

She took off down Rabbit's Run, a twisting trail that led to a saddle between two of the taller ridges. "What a fitting name," she said to herself as she glided down the run. "Rabbit's Run sounds like just the place to begin my new career as a snow bunny."

Finally Enid saw what she was looking for—a boy about her age floundering in the snow for his poles. He had short brown hair and nice, regular features. And snow was lodged in every crevice of his clothing. When he managed to stand up, Enid could see that he was of medium height and build—not spectacularly handsome, but cute.

"Cute's OK," Enid decided aloud, nodding thoughtfully. "I can live with cute."

She took a deep breath and began skiing toward the unsteady young man to offer assistance.

•   •   •

Elizabeth saw a familiar figure skiing ahead of her on Rabbit's Run—a figure in a worn green parka and black ski pants. "Enid!" she called.

Her best friend wheeled around as Elizabeth skied to her. Enid's face was pink—probably from the cold, Elizabeth thought.

"Hi, Enid!" Elizabeth said. "I hope your day has been going better than mine."

Enid didn't answer. Elizabeth followed her gaze, but she saw only a teenage boy wobbling slowly over the snow.

"Are you OK, Enid?" Elizabeth asked. "You were staring off into the distance with a very determined look on your face."

"Oh, I'm fine," Enid said, turning back to Elizabeth. She spoke quickly, as if she was suddenly in a hurry. "I guess you haven't made up with Todd?" she asked.

"Made up with him?" Elizabeth asked. "I've been avoiding him like frostbite. After that stunt he pulled last night, I'm not sure I ever want to speak to him again. Can you believe that he actually thought—" She paused, realizing that Enid was barely listening. "Enid? Are you sure you're all right?"

"I'm fine," Enid repeated. "It's just that I'm in kind of a hurry. There's someone I, uh, was supposed to meet."

Elizabeth looked at her curiously. Enid was a private person in a lot of ways, but it wasn't like her to keep secrets from her best friend. *Whoever Enid's meeting, she sure seems nervous about it,* Elizabeth thought. *Maybe she's met a guy.*

Enid opened her mouth as if she was going to say more, but then she shook her head slightly. "I'll tell you all about it later, Liz. I promise." Again she turned and stared a little way down the slope. Elizabeth watched, too, as the wobbling boy stumbled again. Then a petite blond girl appeared in front of him, as though she'd materialized out of the snow.

"Tony!" the girl called in an amused, loving voice. "I keep telling you—the idea is to stay on top of the snow, not underneath it!" She kissed him on the forehead, placed her hands under his arms with the air of someone who had done it many times before, and helped her boyfriend out of the snow.

Enid sighed deeply and turned back to Elizabeth. "I'm sorry," she said. "What were you saying about Todd?"

A few minutes later Enid left Elizabeth on Rabbit's Run and sped alone down Gerry's Shortcut. It was a difficult run—a black diamond run. But Enid could handle it. And physical exertion had a way of making things come clear in her

88

head. Besides, Gerry's Shortcut would bring her straight down the steep face of the ridge to the Beltway, a green run where she'd be likely to find another uncoordinated male skier.

Enid knew that Elizabeth was concerned about her. But she wasn't quite ready to tell Elizabeth what was on her mind. She hadn't exactly lied to her best friend, she rationalized. She really was planning to meet someone that afternoon. She just didn't know who he was yet.

When Elizabeth first stopped her, Enid had resented the interruption. But now she was grateful to Elizabeth for having saved her from embarrassment. At least she hadn't had time to get out a single sassy word to Tony the cute—but attached—klutz.

Through her pocket, Enid patted her copy of *101 Ways to Be Sassy on the Slopes*. Surely, she thought, there was a klutzy skier out there somewhere who didn't already have a girlfriend. If he was anywhere on the slopes of Snow Mountain, Enid would find him.

Lila's gold watch was covered by the tight-fitting sleeves of her blue parka. But she knew it couldn't be later than three o'clock in the afternoon, despite the fact that she felt as if she'd been skiing up and down the bunny slope for a week.

Then she realized that there was another reason

why it seemed later. The bunny slope was already partly in shadow. Dark clouds were gathering, though the ski patrol was forecasting heavy snows only for the highest elevations. She sighed. Night skiing would probably be canceled for the evening. The afternoon was almost over, and the only action she'd had all day was about fifty runs down the bunny slope, searching for Jessica and Lucas.

But her best friend and the ski instructor were long gone. Lila figured she might as well take the nearest lift up to some real slopes and at least get in a few good runs for the day. She headed east on the Bowling Alley, a low, flat trail that led along the foot of the mountain and which was used for beginning ski classes. Several chairlifts had their starting points along it.

Suddenly a flash of scarlet caught her eye. Lucas's red parka! He and Jessica were sitting on a lift, heading up the mountain. And Jessica was resting her head on his shoulder in a way that made Lila clench her jaw.

Luckily they hadn't seen her. It would take Lucas and Jessica a while to reach the top and to ski down the slope. That gave Lila time to make her plans.

Lila felt the wind blowing through the fur lining of her hood as she sped along the Bowling Alley to the low, gentle slope where Jessica and

Lucas would reach the foot of their ski run. She scouted around to be sure nobody was nearby. Then she gingerly lowered herself to the ground in an awkward pose. She pulled off one ski and tossed it aside. She rubbed some snow into the folds of her French blue ski pants. And she lay back on the snow and arranged her hair to cascade dramatically around her shoulders. Then Lila waited, shivering, for her knight in a shining snowsuit.

Chapter 6

A tall, thin boy was practicing his snowplowing along the run called the Beltway. He wore jeans and an oversized brown parka that looked more like a sleeping bag than a ski jacket. The purplish edge of a knit cap showed on his forehead, beneath his big brown hood.

From a distance, the boy seemed to be about her age, Enid thought. His clumsiness was kind of endearing. She liked the way his arms rotated out of control at his sides, as if he were a character in a cartoon. And the hair that stuck out from under the cap was a perfectly normal shade of brown— not a fluorescent green ponytail in sight. Besides, she'd always had a thing for skinny guys.

Enid began skiing toward the boy at a slow, easy pace. She could dare to be sassy, and she could dare to be a skilled skier. But she wouldn't dare approach another boy before she had taken the time to scope things out. If this one had a nose ring or a girlfriend, Enid wanted to know about it before she made a fool of herself.

Jessica traversed the ridge overlooking the Bowling Alley, forcing herself to keep her speed down to a believable level for her second day on the slopes. Lucas was waiting up ahead, his red parka standing out like a flag against the blue-shadowed snow. She intentionally miscalculated her stop so that she would just slide into him.

"Oops!" she said with a laugh as she grabbed his sides to regain her balance. "Sorry about that."

Lucas flashed her a smile, his teeth whiter than snow. "No problem," he said. "You're doing fine." He gazed into her eyes, and Jessica felt a warm glow spreading through her body. "In fact," Lucas continued, "you've got some great moves."

"So do you," Jessica whispered, her face now very close to his. *This is it!* she thought eagerly. She parted her lips slightly and closed her eyes to receive his kiss.

Suddenly she felt Lucas turn his head away. "Hey!" he cried. "There's your friend, and it looks like she's in trouble!"

He sped away, and Jessica balled her hands into

fists around her ski poles. Lucas was sliding over the packed powder to Lila, who lay in the snow, looking deceptively helpless. Jessica rolled her eyes and followed the ski instructor.

When Jessica skidded to a stop a moment later, Lucas was already helping Lila from the ground and brushing powder from her sleeves.

"Thank you so much, Lucas," Lila gushed. "I don't know what I would have done if you hadn't come along when you did."

"How's the ankle?" Lucas asked. "You fell in kind of an awkward position. I'm surprised the other ski didn't come off, too."

Lila leaned heavily on his arm. She stepped on her right foot and then bit her lip bravely. "Oh, it's just fine," she said with exactly the right amount of pain in her voice. "It's only a sprain."

That's right, Li, Jessica practically said out loud. *Play it for sympathy.* Most guys, she'd observed, were incredibly gullible when they had the chance to believe that women were helpless. She wasn't sure if she should be incensed or impressed with her friend's performance. She settled for both.

"You know, Lila," Lucas said, "I admire your spirit for getting back on the slopes after yesterday. If your ankle weren't giving you so much pain, I'd suggest a joint lesson for you and Jessica tomorrow."

Lila tested her weight on her right foot again.

"Actually, Lucas," she said, "I don't even think it's sprained. I just twisted it a little when I fell. Now that I'm standing on it, it's feeling a lot better."

Jessica rolled her eyes again.

"Well, if you're sure it'll be OK by tomorrow," Lucas said, "I bet I can give you some tips for staying on your feet. In fact, maybe a private lesson would be just the thing. After one day, Jessica is already skiing like a pro. She might want to go off on her own tomorrow, instead of hearing about the same old moves she perfected this morning."

Jessica promptly lost her balance and fell. She grinned sheepishly. "I'm not too sure about that, Lucas," she said, ignoring Lila's glare. "I think I need more lessons." At least a joint lesson would allow her to keep an eye on her so-called best friend.

It was close to four o'clock Sunday afternoon when Elizabeth stepped off the tram at the top of Alpine Peak. Only a few of the heartier athletes were skiing so high up this late in the day. The temperature was dropping, and snow cascaded down in huge, thick flakes like cotton balls.

Elizabeth welcomed the solitude. All day she'd been skiing in the opposite direction every time she saw Todd approaching. He was the better skier, but she banked on being more observant; as long as she saw him coming before he saw her, Elizabeth was sure she could get away. In a way, she knew she was being childish. Certainly they'd have to argue it out sooner or later. But Elizabeth was still too angry for a rational conversation, and she didn't want to fly off the handle at him. She thought that a few difficult runs, in the bracing chill at nine thousand feet might help freeze the edge off her ire. She was sure that by dinnertime she would be able to handle the confrontation that seemed inevitable.

Luckily she hadn't seen Todd lately. Maybe he'd finally given up trying to talk to her on the slopes.

Elizabeth selected Snowbird Run, which had seemed so pretty in the semidarkness of the night before, and pushed off through the rapidly falling snow. She gasped at the beauty of one of the few clumps of pine trees at this altitude. They must have been very tall trees, but only their tops were visible over the snow. The boughs were swathed in crystal snowflakes that shimmered like stars.

If it weren't so cold, I'd sit down and write a poem right here, she said to herself. Instead she memorized the image of the snow-laden treetops against the white mountainside and gray sky. She would write about it later in her journal.

She hit a mogul field and delighted in the vibrations that ran through her skis and into her legs as she sailed over bump after bump. Moguls could be tricky to navigate, but she felt totally confident, keeping her center of balance forward and her knees supple. There was nothing like a good workout to help her forget her problems. The outrage of the night before dissipated as Elizabeth gloried in the feeling of being alive and strong and free.

She glided onto a smooth, level section of the run and slowed her pace so that she could catch her breath. Suddenly she heard the whirring of skis on snow behind her. She pulled aside to let the faster skier pass. But the other skier turned expertly and stopped directly in front of her. It was a boy her age in a hunter green parka.

"Todd," she said in a flat voice. She was in love with Todd and had been for ages. But she had never been so disappointed to see him.

"Please, Liz," he said. "I've been trying to talk to you all day."

"I'd rather talk this evening," Elizabeth said, trying to keep her voice calm. "I'm enjoying my solitude right now."

"Elizabeth, this can't wait!" Todd insisted.

"That's just it!" she screamed, unable to hold her frustration in any longer. "That was the problem last night, too! You couldn't wait!"

"Liz—"

"I always expected more from you than that!" Elizabeth cried. "I trusted you! But what about my feelings? You didn't even ask me what I wanted last night! You just assumed that I would want whatever you wanted. Well, I didn't! And right now I don't want to talk. I said I'd discuss it with you this evening, so you'll just have to wait until then."

Todd was standing directly in her path, so Elizabeth executed a turn and sped off to one side, leaving the groomed ski run behind.

"Elizabeth!" Todd called from behind her. "You're skiing away from the trail! Come back, please! The snow conditions aren't safe!"

Elizabeth ignored his voice, which quickly thinned and was carried away by the gathering wind. She was a perfectly good skier, and she could take care of herself.

Todd had been right about one thing, she decided a few minutes later. Skiing conditions were bad. Less than an hour earlier, she'd felt soaring confidence as she bounced over moguls. Now every bump in her path jarred her entire body. She turned to see how far she'd come, but the snow was falling thickly now, whirling like Van Gogh's stars. And she couldn't see even the faintest sign of Todd's hunter green parka behind her.

Well, that's just fine, she decided silently. *I'll concentrate on skiing back to the tram, and I won't give another thought to Todd until I'm at the lodge, sipping a hot chocolate.*

Elizabeth peered around her again. She thought she saw a red blur out of the corner of her eye, but it disappeared into the blowing white. She gauged the sun's position by a whiter kind of glow in one place on the horizon. Then she took a deep breath and decided that the tram was in the opposite direction, to the east.

Enid skied skillfully along the Beltway, making sure that her technique was perfect. She wanted to impress the klutzy skier in the brown coat, but she had to keep her speed slow enough so that she wouldn't intimidate him.

Guys had an ego thing about being less athletic than women. She knew she had a fine line to slalom between helping the guy and showing him up. Well, tact was something Enid was good at. She would blame his problems on everything from his equipment to the weather rather than suggest that his skiing prowess wasn't up to par. She thought that most boys could deal with being helped by a girl—as long as they were allowed to save face.

Enid took a deep breath, put a sassy smile on her face, and skied closer. She'd watched the tall, skinny skier long enough to know that he was alone. His back was turned to her, so she couldn't tell for sure about the nose ring. But he didn't seem like the type.

"Hi there!" she called to his brown-jacketed back. "You look like you're having a little trouble with the, um, snow conditions. Can I help?"

"Yeah, the snow conditions," the boy said quickly. "That's exactly the problem." Then he fell flat on his face.

"Everyone knows that this kind of snow is especially hard to ski in," Enid said as she pulled off her own skis to help him up. "Maybe I can give you some tips."

She reached down to grab his arm—and looked right into the face of Winston Egbert.

"Winston!" she exclaimed.

"Enid!" he exclaimed, his face turning red.

Inwardly Enid cursed her own tendency to blush lavishly. She was sure she looked as if she were wearing hot-pink sunblock all over her face. But she was puzzled. Surely Winston was a great skier. She could have sworn she'd seen him skiing on past trips. There must be some other explanation for his clumsiness.

"Are you all right?" she asked, desperately hoping he didn't realize that she'd been trying to pick him up.

"Oh, I'm fine," Winston said quickly, stumbling to his feet. "Indestructible, really. It's, uh, these rental skis," he said, gesturing toward the skis that lay in the snow nearby.

"I thought you said it was the snow conditions," Enid said absently. But she was really trying to determine if he was mortified because she'd caught him falling down or if he was uncomfortable because of her feeble attempt to get sassy with him.

"Yes, it *is* the snow conditions," Winston said, "combined with the skis. They're a different size than my own skis, and I'm not used to them."

"Why didn't you just bring your own skis on the trip?" Enid asked. As she spoke, she was thinking desperately: *I didn't have a chance to say anything that would make him think I'm trying to seduce him or anything . . . did I?*

Winston shrugged. "My brother borrowed them," he said quickly.

"Winston, you don't have a brother," Enid pointed out mechanically. Meanwhile her mind raced to remember everything she *had* said before she'd recognized Winston.

"Oh, did I say brother?" Winston laughed. "I meant cousin. My cousin borrowed them. He asked me ages ago, before this trip was planned. So I figured I'd rent some here."

Enid began to relax. Winston sounded manic, but it apparently didn't have anything to do with her—she hoped. She picked up a ski and measured it against his height. "Well, these rental skis seem to be the perfect length for you, Winston. You shouldn't be having a problem."

"You know how it is," he said glibly. "Once you're used to something, you really like it better, even if it isn't exactly the way it's supposed to be. It's kind of like people who get used to drinking that nasty diet soda—"

"You're babbling, Winston," Enid told him, amused. "Besides, I get the picture." *I get it, all right,* she thought with an inward laugh. *Winston can't ski!* And he didn't want his friends to know it.

"Babbling?" Winston asked. "Yes, I suppose I am. But what the heck, everyone needs a hobby."

"Maybe you should try taking up skiing next," she suggested.

"You know, Enid, you may be on to something." He had a resigned look on his face, as if he'd realized that she knew his secret.

Enid wanted to tell him not to worry, that she wouldn't say anything to the others about his lack of skiing ability, but she didn't get the chance. Winston reached out to pat her on the shoulder in the one-of-the-guys kind of gesture that boys tended to adopt with her. But he lost his balance, knocked into Enid, and sent them both sprawling in the snow.

"Oops," Winston said, looking like a skinny,

snowy grizzly bear in his brown coat. He reached out a hand to help her up, but Enid refused it. It seemed safer that way. "Sorry about that, Enid," Winston said. "Oh, something fell out of your pocket. Let me get that for you."

"No!" Enid cried, but she was too late. Winston picked up her new book and shook the snowflakes from its cover.

"*A Hundred and One Ways to Be Sassy on the Slopes,*" he read as he handed the book to her. An incredulous look spread across his face. "What is this?"

"Just a book," Enid said with a laugh, silently cursing the tricky zipper on her parka pocket.

"It doesn't seem like your usual choice of reading matter," Winston said, his face turning as red as hers felt.

If the Olympics had a competitive blushing event, Winston and I would be top contenders, Enid thought wryly.

"It was a gag gift," she lied glibly, hoping to convince him that of course she would never take such a book seriously. *Oh, brilliant,* she told herself. *Everyone carries gag gifts they don't take seriously around in their pockets when they ski.* Winston was the class clown, for heaven's sake—not the village idiot.

"Oh," he said kindly. "A gag gift. Yep, that's a pretty good gag."

A look passed between them, and Enid knew they had a contract—*You keep my secret, and I'll keep yours.* But both were too embarrassed to talk about it. For now, it would be easier to pretend that neither knew the other was hiding a thing.

"By the way, Winston," she added, "your nose is peeling. I've got a whole extra stick of sunblock that you can have. It's practically brand-new—only used once!"

"Sunblock?" Winston asked, a confused look fleeting across his face. "Yeah, thanks," he said, accepting the lime green stick. "I guess I did forget mine."

Todd watched helplessly while Elizabeth skied off into the rapidly falling snow. He wrapped his arms around himself and shivered, as much from the icy blast of her tirade as from the increasing chill in the air.

Suddenly a glint of red caught his eye. He turned just in time to see the woman in the bright red ski suit—the one who had asked him to be her lift partner. He considered calling out to her to warn her about the storm and the unsafe conditions on the far side of the mountain, where she seemed to be heading. But she was gone before he had the chance. He decided he'd let the ski patrol know she was out there, as soon as he made it back to the tram.

Todd didn't really think that the woman in red was in much danger. She was obviously a strong skier—she could have been a pro. Her technique wasn't as graceful as Elizabeth's, he decided, but she seemed more athletic.

When he thought of his girlfriend, a warning flag went up in Todd's head. Elizabeth was a good skier, but snow conditions off-trail were bad at this high altitude. And the storm wouldn't make things any easier for her. He debated with himself about going after her. She had a head start, of course. But she wasn't strong enough to move quickly through the wet, lumpy snow. He knew he was a faster skier.

Maybe it wasn't such a good idea to follow her. The tram wasn't far away. Surely Elizabeth could find her way there safely; the storm wasn't really that bad yet. And there was another consideration he couldn't brush aside. Some girls—Jessica and Lila, for instance, when it suited their twisted motives—loved playing the damsel in distress, dependent on big, strong men to rescue them. Not Elizabeth. She was angry enough with him already. If she thought that he thought she needed his help to ski a few hundred yards—well, one tirade per night was about all that Todd could handle.

On the other hand, if there was even a chance that Elizabeth could get lost or hurt, then he had

105

no choice but to follow her—even if she refused to speak to him for the rest of the week.

Todd gauged the depth of the newly fallen snow with the edge of one ski. He took a deep breath and noted that the air had gotten colder in the last few minutes. And it seemed darker than it should have been at four o'clock in the afternoon, even in the mountains. But something else in the air alarmed him more—a sense of uneasy anticipation, as if something huge and terrible were waiting to pounce.

Todd made up his mind. He set out quickly in the direction Elizabeth had gone.

It was still early in the evening, but the mountain air seemed a lot colder to Jessica once her all-day lesson with Lucas was over. Now she was sitting in the restaurant, warm and comfortable in a low-cut sweater and black jeans, sipping a hot chocolate and waiting for Lila to share an early dinner. She was still angry at her best friend for manipulating Lucas into turning the next day's lesson into a joint one. But when Jessica remembered how close she had come to kissing him at the foot of the mountain, she knew it was only a matter of time. Lila or no Lila, Lucas was hers.

"Hey, Jessica," Lila called, sliding into the seat across from her. She conspicuously shoved a large shopping bag onto the table between them. Jessica knew her friend well enough to know that Lila was dying to have her ask what was in the bag. But Jessica was determined to act as if she didn't care.

"Ice Breakers?" Jessica asked in a slightly bored tone, reading the store name on the bag. "What's that?"

Lila shrugged. "It's the women's ski boutique on the other side of the lodge," she said nonchalantly. "Oh, I guess you haven't been to that one. It's really for guests who are shopping in the *higher* price ranges."

"No, I guess not," Jessica admitted sarcastically, trying to hide her curiosity about Lila's latest purchase. "I buy all my ski clothes at the Salvation Army Ski Shop."

"Oh, Jessica, you're so funny," Lila said. Her mouth was laughing, Jessica noted, but her eyes were not amused.

"So what did you buy?" Jessica asked, and immediately wanted to kick herself. She hadn't meant to show any interest, but the question had slipped out somehow.

Lila grinned triumphantly, and Jessica knew she'd lost a skirmish in the Battle of Snow Mountain.

"I saw someone I didn't expect at the boutique," Lila began in a conversational tone, taking much longer than necessary to open the bag.

Jessica knew exactly what was happening: Now that Lila had Jessica in suspense, she was stalling to prolong the agony.

"Who?" Jessica asked, hoping Lila would answer quickly and then get on with it.

"Enid Rollins!"

Jessica was interested despite herself. "Enid? In a fancy designer ski shop? What on earth was she buying?"

Lila shrugged. "I couldn't say," she replied, already losing interest in the subject. "Enid was walking in as I was leaving. We'll have to keep an eye on what she's wearing this week."

"Whatever it is, it's got to be an improvement over that ancient green thing I saw her in today," Jessica said. "But you know Enid. She's more concerned about being practical than about being seen. Talk about mixed-up priorities!"

From the shopping bag, Lila pulled out the edge of a tissue-wrapped package. "And now, the moment you've been waiting for," she said with a smug smile. "This is just a little something I picked up to wear for Lucas."

I'd like to give her a little something, Jessica thought, her hand balling into a fist under the table. "Good idea," she said in a nonchalant tone. "You really ought to have one ski outfit that doesn't make you look fat."

Lila's eyebrows shot up for just an instant, and Jessica clapped her hands together under the table. This time, Jessica knew, she was the one who had scored.

"Wait until you see this," Lila gushed, unwrapping the tissue paper. "You are just going to die!"

She pulled part of a one-piece ski suit from its wrappings, and Jessica couldn't keep her fingers from stroking the soft fabric. It was pure, dazzling white, shot through with silver threads. From what Jessica could see, it was both elegant and sexy, like most of Lila's better purchases. *And it probably cost about as much as my Jeep!* Jessica gritted her teeth and tallied another loss on the Wakefield side of her mental scorecard. She hadn't come to this war fully armed. All she had were brains and sex appeal. Lila's credit cards might prove to be much more useful weapons.

Elizabeth skied on, plowing through the heavy, mushy snow and wishing she had snowshoes, or at least cross-country skis. The terrain and weather conditions were horrendous—and quickly getting worse. She stopped a minute to look around her. Had she come far enough to have reached the tram by now? Had she overshot it somehow?

No, she decided. *I'm fine.* She'd just been moving somewhat more slowly than she'd originally estimated.

The wind and the slope of the mountain had pushed her off course a little. She turned her skis to the left and plodded on, slowly and deliberately, toward the tram.

Suddenly a dark green blur shot past her, and Elizabeth recognized Todd's parka. "Darn him!" she muttered, turning too quickly toward the glimpse of green. Distracted, she slipped and fell as he sped by. Obviously Todd hadn't seen her. But now he was shooting down the far side of the mountain—away from the tram, Elizabeth was sure.

"He couldn't trust *me* to be a good enough skier to make it back by myself," Elizabeth fumed as she picked herself up from the snow. "But *he*'s not even headed in the right direction! Todd may be a better skier than I am, but I've got a better sense of direction any day. I swear, he could get lost trying to find—"

Suddenly a sickening rumble knocked the world off balance. A noise like thunder filled the air; the mountain vibrated with it. Then the ground shifted beneath her, and Elizabeth felt as if she were tumbling a tremendous distance—through darkness, and in slow motion. An instant later she was face down in the cold, wet snow.

For a moment Elizabeth remembered a minor earthquake she'd felt back home in California. But this was different—scarier and more confusing.

And the worst of the thunderous roar emanated from the far side of the mountain, where Todd had just disappeared into the swirling snow.

"Todd!" Elizabeth screamed.

There was no answer. But the rumbling stopped abruptly, to be replaced by a horrible, expectant stillness.

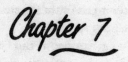

Chapter 7

Elizabeth could feel her heart pounding through the thick fiberfill layers of her parka. She tried to take deep, slow breaths. "Don't panic," she breathed, repeating the phrase like a mantra. "Don't panic."

She struggled to a sitting position in the snow and took stock of the situation. There had been an avalanche on one part of the mountain; that much seemed clear. At least she wasn't hurt. The ground had given way beneath her, and she'd slid partway down the slope. But that small shift in the snow must have been caused by the vibrations coming from the eastern side of the mountain, where tons of ice and snow had exploded from the ridge and cascaded downward.

And she had last seen Todd racing east, looking for her.

"Todd!" she called again into the falling snow, not expecting an answer. Fear and panic gripped her. Todd had been caught in the avalanche. And it was all her fault.

Elizabeth's ski poles had disappeared. Her skis had fallen off when she'd tumbled down the slope, but they lay nearby, partly buried in the snow. She fished them out and fought her way to a standing position in the wet snow. The skis wouldn't help her scale the ridge she had just fallen down. But she might need them later, to reach the ski patrol station near the tram as quickly as possible.

Todd might be hurt or trapped somewhere—*or worse,* added an insistent voice in her mind. "No!" she cried. That was too horrible to contemplate. For now, she had to believe that Todd was alive. But if he was out there on the eastern slope of Alpine Peak, he might be in need of help. And she was the only one who knew that he was there.

She had to get help for him. She just had to. She threw the skis over one shoulder and began picking her way, sobbing, up the slippery hill.

Enid checked her wristwatch. She was sitting with Winston, Olivia, and Caroline at the ski resort's restaurant. It was still early, but she'd assumed that Elizabeth and Todd would be back from the slopes by now, too.

113

"Maybe they wanted to be alone," Caroline suggested, a knowing smile on her face.

Uh-oh, Enid thought. *Caroline's got her gossip antenna out. We'll have to be very careful about what we say. Elizabeth and Todd wouldn't want the whole school to know what happened last night.* She exchanged glances with Winston and Olivia. Both of them knew about Todd and Elizabeth's argument, and both nodded almost imperceptibly, agreeing to cover for their friends.

Winston brushed some snow from his hair. "I don't know if Todd and Liz specifically wanted to be alone this evening," he began. "They were probably just having such a good time skiing that they lost track of the time."

"Speaking of leaving Todd and Elizabeth alone," Caroline began slyly, "late last night I saw you on the couch in the lobby, Winston. Why in the world were you sleeping there?"

Olivia laughed. "Win and I were sitting by the fireplace, playing Trivial Pursuit, and he fell fast asleep, right in the middle of a question about the French and Indian War," she said quickly. "Personally, I think it was a defense mechanism. He knew I was winning."

"I bet you tried for fifteen minutes to wake me up, too," Winston said with a hollow laugh. "My mother always says the Sweet Valley High marching band could parade through my bedroom in the morning and I wouldn't even turn over."

"That's right," Olivia said. "Finally I gave up and let him sleep there. I figured he'd wake up sooner or later and go back to his own room."

"Oh," Caroline said, looking disappointed. "But I still think there's something going on between Elizabeth and Todd. I can't decide if they're mad at each other or if they're being sneaky to throw us off the track."

Olivia shrugged. "I don't think there's anything unusual going on," she said. "Liz told me a little while ago that she was looking for him so they could discuss their ski plans for tomorrow. They wanted to test out some new runs. I think Todd's working up to ski Devil's Run by the end of the week."

"I've been thinking of doing the same thing myself," Enid added, steering the subject away from Elizabeth and Todd. "What about you, Winston? You looked pretty good slaloming down the slopes this afternoon."

Winston smiled gratefully. "I was planning to try Devil's Run," he said. "But my trick knee has been acting up. I might have to skip the black diamond areas this week and make do with the boring old green runs."

"That's probably best," Enid agreed.

After a waiter took their order, Winston launched into a totally fabricated story about his skiing adventures throughout the day. As he spoke, Enid watched her friend thoughtfully. Now that Winston knew what she was really after, he might be a valuable ally in her attempts to find romance on the slopes.

Enid had tried Method Three that afternoon— yelling "Single!" in the lift line to indicate that she needed someone to share a chair with. The book promised that good-looking ski bums would instantly materialize and fight for the chance to sit with her. Instead a jovial man of about her father's age had stepped up, perfectly innocently, introduced himself as Gerald Trainor, and offered to be her seatmate. Enid had actually had a great time listening to his stories of Killington and Lake Placid and his lusty rendition of "If I Were a Rich Man." But it hadn't brought her any closer to picking up a ski bum of her very own.

"Is that thunder in the distance?" Olivia asked suddenly, interrupting Enid's thoughts. "What a long, low rumble!"

Winston shrugged. "The ski patrol was expecting some kind of freaky storm on the far side of the mountain, way up near the top. I hear it's not unusual to get electrical storms with snow around here in the early spring." He continued with a story about racing down Snowbird Run against a guy who had almost been an alternate for the U.S. Olympic team, and Enid went back to her assessment of her progress toward becoming a snow bunny.

She had Method Four under control. It involved wearing cool shades, and she'd just bought a pair of purple-tinted goggles in an overpriced boutique called Ice Breakers. She would try them out the next day.

Method Five was hanging out in the lodge disco at night and asking a cute ski bum to dance. *I'm definitely going to try it tonight,* she repeated to herself, nervous but determined. Asking strangers to dance was not Enid's usual style, but she thought it was about time for her to come out of her shell and be more sociable.

She might need Winston's help when she got to Method Six: showing an interest in the local professional sports teams. Enid was as athletic as the next person. But except for Sweet Valley High teams, she wasn't much of a sports spectator. She knew enough about football to bluff her way through a discussion of the Broncos' Super Bowl chances. But football season was long over. And she didn't know a thing about major league baseball.

"You're putting us on, Winston," Caroline insisted. "There's no way you could beat a guy who was almost an alternate for the Olympic team. I saw you skiing the Bowling Alley this morning, and the only thing you were beating was your face against the ground!"

"That's because you saw him in the morning," Enid interjected. She figured Winston would be more willing to help her if she covered for him. "I saw Winston later in the day, and we figured out that the rental desk had given him the wrong size skis. The proper equipment makes such a difference, you know," she concluded. "As soon as Winston was wearing a shorter pair of skis, he was off like lightning."

"There's more of that weird thunder," Olivia said. She folded her arms in front of her, as if she were cold. "It kind of gives me the creeps. I hope Elizabeth and Todd are at a low enough elevation to be out of the bad weather."

Winston shrugged. "I wouldn't worry about it. They're both excellent skiers."

Panting, Elizabeth threw herself onto the level top of the ridge of snow she'd just climbed. She was sweating under her thick ski clothes. But at the same time she was shivering from the cold—and from fear. Gusts of wind hurled stinging particles of snow and sleet at her, chapping her face and making her teeth chatter. But the only thing that mattered was reaching the ski patrol and sending a search party out after Todd.

Suddenly the ground vibrated, and the mountain itself seemed to roar. Elizabeth screamed and scrambled to regain her footing. For an instant she thought she was about to plummet back down the hillside she'd just struggled so hard to conquer. But she kept her balance. Then the rumbling subsided, leaving only a faint echo that reverberated throughout her body.

She was exhausted but frantic. Darkness was descending quickly, and she somehow knew for certain that Todd was in danger. She forced herself to conserve energy by pacing herself as she trudged through the deep snow in the direction of the aerial tram and the ski patrol.

Todd wasn't sure exactly what had happened, but in all the years he had been skiing, he'd never wiped out in such a big way. He had a vague memory of losing his balance, as if the ground had lurched beneath his skis. He could remember a swirl of gray and blue and white, with chunks of snow and ice ramming into him from every side. Now Todd was partly buried in the stuff, and the cold was seeping through his clothes. He thought he might have been unconscious for a minute or two. His head was throbbing so hard that a concussion seemed like a distinct possibility. He wrenched his body out from under the snow, his muscles about as sore as if he'd just finished all four rounds of the state basketball championship.

Along with his skis and poles, Todd's sunglasses were gone. He used one hand to shield his eyes against the snow's glare, so that he could get his bearings. He blinked. The terrain looked completely different from the landscape he'd been skiing through only minutes earlier. It wasn't just that his own position had shifted a little. He knew that the tram lay somewhere west of him. West was toward the glow of the sun that still hung low in the sky. But the entire shape of the mountain was transformed, and he was standing near the edge of a vast spill of ice and snow that towered above him and completely cut off his path back to the western slopes.

Suddenly Todd knew exactly what had caused his fall and reshaped the landscape. A sick feeling of fear gripped him. Where was Elizabeth?

"Elizabeth!" he called, surprised at the weakness of his voice against the vast stillness. He stumbled toward the sprawl of hard snow and ice, panic shooting through his body. "Elizabeth!"

The panic gripped him more powerfully than the pain in his head and limbs. Elizabeth could be buried under tons of snow and ice. She could be trapped, alone and afraid in the frigid air. She could be dying.

"Over here!" called a female voice.

Todd whirled, expecting to see Elizabeth's familiar blond hair and navy parka. Instead he saw a black-haired woman in a scarlet ski suit pointing toward a tiny cabin that was practically buried in the snow. It was the woman in red—the thirtyish woman he'd seen near the chairlift the evening before and again just before the avalanche. She must have been caught on the edge of the slide, just as he was. And from where Todd stood, a hundred feet away, she didn't seem to be hurt, either.

Suddenly a roar like thunder nearly knocked Todd off his feet. Another hunk of ice and snow had just cascaded off the side of the mountain, somewhere nearby. The earth seemed to vibrate beneath him for several seconds afterward.

Well, I can't stay here, he realized. *And I can't get back to the tram through that mess.* It seemed that his only option was to follow the woman in red to shelter—and to pray that Elizabeth was all right.

Elizabeth pushed desperately toward the ski patrol station, plowing through the thick, wet snow that slowed her progress and gummed up her skis. It was dusk, and grainy snow was still falling, pelting her like pebbles. She nearly doubled over from the sharp pain that stabbed through her lungs with every icy breath. She was driving herself too hard, she knew. But she had no choice. She had to get help.

Finally she saw the red tram car in the distance. And next door to the tram depot was a log cabin with a sign out front: SUMMIT STATION, SNOW MOUNTAIN SKI PATROL.

121

Elizabeth fumbled for the doorknob, cursing her numb hands. The door opened from the inside, and Elizabeth practically fell into the building, stumbling past a tall, well-built young man in a black-and-red ski patrol uniform. She collapsed into a chair, trying to catch her breath.

"An avalanche!" she choked out, pointing wildly in the direction where she thought Todd had gone. "Need help—"

The man who had opened the door crouched in front of her, his hand on her arm. "We know about the avalanche," he told her in a soft Southern drawl. He looked about twenty-five years old and had sandy blond hair. "Were you caught in it? Are you hurt?"

"No!" Elizabeth screamed, still panting and shivering. "Not m-m-me!"

The man turned to a petite, redheaded patrol member who sat at a desk nearby. "Donna, get us a couple of blankets here," he ordered. Then he squeezed Elizabeth's hand. "I'm Dirk Roman," he said. "I'm head of the ski patrol for Alpine Peak. I want you to stop and take a couple of deep breaths and then tell me who you are and what happened to you out there."

Elizabeth nodded, grateful for his kindness and calm strength. Meanwhile Donna draped a blanket around her shoulders. Dirk helped Elizabeth pull off her gloves and then handed her a steaming cup of tea.

"Don't drink it too fast," he told her gently.

Elizabeth didn't think she could down even a sip, but she was thankful for the warmth of the ceramic mug against her reddened fingers. "I'm—I'm Elizabeth Wakefield," she panted. "A-a-and you've got to send out a search party! He was caught out there in the avalanche, and it's all my fault!"

Dirk turned to another ski patrol member. "Nick, put in a radio call down to Beltway Station," he ordered. "Have them start preparing a rescue party to supplement the staff we have on hand here. I want a crew ready by dawn."

"*Dawn?*" Elizabeth screamed. "He could be dead by then!"

"Shhh," Dirk said in a soft, soothing voice that she could barely hear over a sudden burst of static on the two-way radio that Dirk's colleague was using at Donna's desk. "We can't search in the dark," Dirk continued. "And the sun's already setting. But I already did send out a party—just after the avalanche occurred, to report back on any damage. Chances are they'll find your friend within the next few minutes and will head straight back here with him." He reached up to pull Elizabeth's hood off her head. Despite the cold, her forehead was slick with sweat. "So tell me exactly what happened, Elizabeth. Who is out there?"

"His name is Todd Wilkins," she said brokenly.

"He's sixteen years old, and I saw him skiing toward the east face just a few minutes before the avalanche. He must have been caught in it! You have to help him, *please!*"

"Donna," Dirk called behind him without turning away from Elizabeth, "are there any reports of a sixteen-year-old boy showing up here at the station or at the tram depot in the last hour?"

"I'm afraid not," replied the redhead. "And the tram stopped running just before the avalanche, because of the weather conditions. So he couldn't have headed back down already."

Dirk nodded. "All right, Donna. Then begin preparing our own search party for tomorrow morning with all the usual equipment—avalanche protocol. Elizabeth, you can help Todd by answering some questions for me. First, what kind of a skier is your friend?"

"Really good," Elizabeth told him through the tears that were beginning to slide down her face once more. "He can handle the black diamond runs with no problem."

"Good," Dirk replied. "An expert stands a much better chance out there in an avalanche. But do you know why he was skiing over there? He should have known that it was a restricted area this afternoon, because of the weather and snow conditions."

Elizabeth nodded tearfully. "I know," she

124

sobbed. "But it was all m-m-my fault. We, um, had an argument and I ran away from the trail without thinking about it, and he was following me. B-but he didn't see me, and he went too far."

Dirk's handsome features were set in a concerned frown. "Elizabeth, you can't blame yourself for this," he said, his hands on her shoulders. "No matter what you said or did, an avalanche is an act of nature. If your friend has been hurt, it's because he had the bad luck to be on the wrong side of the mountain when the slide began. It's not your fault."

"What if he's injured or trapped under the snow?" Elizabeth cried. "What if he's d-d-dead?" She fell forward, collapsing into Dirk Roman's strong arms.

"Your friend has probably dug himself a nice, cozy den in the snow, and right now I bet he's eating a Power Bar and waiting to be rescued," Dirk assured her. He lowered his voice. "But Tony," he called to the other patrol officer, "just in case he isn't, I want you to radio the main station at the lodge and be sure there's an ambulance on standby below when we get him out of here."

Elizabeth's sobs intensified, and Dirk's arms tightened around her, giving her support and comfort.

Todd and the woman in red scooped out the last few armfuls of snow from a space directly in front of the log cabin near the avalanche field. "That should do it," Todd called over the wind's howls. "Even with snow still covering the bottom half, I think I can get the door open now."

"It's a good thing it opens inward," the woman replied. She also was raising her voice to be heard, but it still sounded as low and throaty as it had the day before, reminding him of a cat purring.

Todd tried the doorknob, but it seemed to be jammed. "This place must have been built for stranded skiers like us," he shouted. "So it couldn't be locked. I bet it's frozen shut!"

"Try brute force," she suggested, her gaze suggesting that she was sizing up his arms and shoulders. "I bet you're strong enough."

Todd nodded and then rammed his shoulder against the door, sending shock waves screaming through every sore muscle in his body. The door didn't budge.

"Here, I'll help," said the woman. She stood directly behind him, so that the front of her body barely grazed his back. They planted their feet firmly in the snow and then, together, pushed against the door. Finally it gave way. The door swung open so fast that Todd and the black-haired woman tumbled inside and fell three feet to the level of the floor.

They were sprawled on wooden planks in the center of a dim twenty-by-twenty room with some built-in cabinets and a few pieces of rough wooden furniture—a table, a twin-size bed, and a vinyl-covered couch.

The woman rose to her knees, laughing. "I'm Cassandra Lee," she said, reaching out to shake his hand. She stood and pulled her skis and poles through the doorway. Then she watched with dark, intense eyes as Todd jumped up and shut the door with a bang against the three-foot-high wall of snow that still blocked its lower half.

Cassandra was nearly twice his age, but she was a beautiful woman, Todd had to admit. Her scarlet ski suit hugged the curves of her hourglass figure, and the disarray of her glossy black hair only made her look sexier. But her insistent gaze made Todd feel uneasy, as if she was imagining what he looked like underneath his ski clothes. Not that he had anything against attractive women. But it seemed inappropriate in their grim situation.

"I, uh, think we should take stock of what we've got here," Todd began in a businesslike tone. He unzipped his parka, but he didn't take it off. Even in the cabin, he could see his breath on the air.

"An excellent idea," Cassandra said. "I'll show you what I've got if you'll show me what you've got."

For an instant Todd's eyebrows shot up to the middle of his forehead. *Is this woman coming on to me?* Then he exhaled slowly as Cassandra

127

began emptying the small waterproof pack she wore around her waist. Obviously he was reading too much into every gesture. *It'd be a lot easier not to,* he thought, *if she weren't so attractive.*

"Matches," she said, pulling out a packet and flicking it onto the wooden table in the center of the room. "And cigarettes—though I suppose you don't smoke."

Todd shook his head and immediately regretted it. The motion left him reeling, his headache intensified.

Cassandra pulled out two granola bars. "And these," she added. "That's it, unless you count my wallet, lip balm, and hairbrush. How about you?"

Todd shook his head again, more gingerly this time. "Not a thing except my lift pass and a twenty-dollar bill," he said, "for all the good either one will do us here. But this place must be stocked with supplies."

The cabin consisted of a single large room. There was no plumbing or electricity, but a lean-to built onto the back contained a latrine-style toilet. A fireplace on one wall was equipped with a cast-iron grate and poker, firewood was stacked against the wall, and Cassandra found a supply of candles and more matches in a corner cabinet, along with an oil lamp.

"Food!" Todd cried, opening the other corner cabinet. "This one has a few canned goods, and a can opener, and plates. And there's bottled water and some granola bars, and a couple of packages of those peanut-butter crackers."

"Well, that will easily keep us going for the night," Cassandra said, lighting the oil lamp and placing it on the table. "And by tomorrow someone will surely be by to get us out of here—"

"Oh, wow!" Todd cried, catching sight of a headset and receiver on a shelf in the corner. "That's a radio set!"

"As in Top Forty and country-western?" Cassandra asked.

"No," he said, leaping across the cabin and pulling on the headset. "As in two-way communications. It's a CB radio. We can use it to alert the ski patrol that we're out here!"

"Do you know how to do that?" Cassandra asked.

Todd shrugged. "I'm no expert, but I think I can manage," he said, fiddling with the dial. A burst of static was replaced by a hum of hollow-sounding, not-quite-understandable voices. "Hello!" Todd shouted into the headset's microphone. He winced at the pain in his head. "I'm stranded in a cabin on the east face of Alpine Peak," he announced in a quieter voice. "Can anybody hear me? Please respond!"

Chapter 8

Elizabeth fidgeted on the couch in the ski patrol station Sunday evening, watching Dirk and the other patrol members finalize their search plan for the following morning. The initial patrol had returned with a report on the size and exact location of the avalanche. They had even found the ski poles that Elizabeth had lost in her fall. But they hadn't found Todd.

Dirk stood in front of a large contour map of Alpine Peak, using a pointer to show the leaders of the two rescue teams where their parties would search in the morning. Suddenly a burst of static from the radio on Donna's desk caught Elizabeth's attention.

"Please respond if you read me," came a tinny male voice. From the weary inflection, it was clear that the speaker had been repeating the line for some time.

Elizabeth leaped to her feet. "That's Todd!" she screamed.

Dirk was at the radio in an instant, with Elizabeth right beside him.

"Todd Wilkins?" Dirk asked into the microphone, hurriedly adjusting the speaker so that Elizabeth could hear, too. "This is the ski patrol, Summit Station. Are you injured? Can you give me your location?"

Todd's voice replied, but most of his words were lost in another growl of static. "We're fine" was all that Elizabeth could make out.

"We?" Elizabeth asked aloud. "Who's 'we'?"

"Todd?" Dirk repeated. "Todd?"

Todd's voice swelled, but Elizabeth still couldn't understand what he was saying. Then the sound faded, and the radio went silent.

Dirk twirled the knobs on the machine but got nothing more. "It sounds like that's all we're going to hear from Todd tonight," he said to Elizabeth in his soft, soothing drawl. "Either his radio's gone dead or the storm is interfering with communications. At least we know that they're alive and well."

"But we still don't know where he is!" Elizabeth cried. "And what did he mean by 'we'? Todd was alone when he passed me on the mountain."

Dirk shrugged. "There's no way to tell," he said. "Maybe he met up with someone else who was also stranded by the avalanche. We'll put a call into the lodge to see if anyone else has been reported missing."

"As for where they are," Donna suggested, pointing to several small brown squares on Dirk's map, "we've got nearly a dozen small cabins scattered around the mountain. They're supplied with a little food and some firewood—and a CB radio. My guess is that your friend and whoever he's with have made their way to one of them."

"That's my guess, too," Dirk said. "Three of those cabins are in proximity to the avalanche area. So that's where we'll start the search tomorrow."

"Tomorrow?" Elizabeth asked. "We can't leave him out there in the wilderness all night! We just can't!"

Dirk smiled sympathetically. "I know how you feel, Elizabeth, but we don't have any choice. The sun is already down. It's too dark."

"But I have to see him tonight!" Elizabeth said in a low, determined voice. "I have to tell him I'm sorry."

Todd slammed his fist into his palm and stared at the radio set as if it were a television. "Come in, ski patrol!" he yelled into the microphone. "Please come in!"

But all the radio emitted was static. The only other response was the sharp throbbing of Todd's head.

"Worthless piece of junk!" he yelled, banging on the radio.

Cassandra laughed. "Isn't that just like a man," she observed. "If something's broken, hit it as hard as you can. Very effective repair technique."

"I have to find out if Elizabeth's all right," Todd said insistently. "She was out there somewhere, alone."

"Elizabeth?" Cassandra asked. "Is that your girlfriend?"

Todd nodded.

"Well, if it helps any, I'm pretty sure I saw her a few minutes before the avalanche," Cassandra said. "She wasn't too far away, but she was definitely on the west side of the peak. So she's probably fine."

"But I looked for her there!" Todd insisted. "I didn't see her!"

Cassandra shrugged. "It's a big mountain. Besides, Elizabeth wasn't the only one who was out on it when the avalanche roared by. You and I were both out there, too. And we're fine—relatively speaking. If we managed to get through it OK, she probably did, too. Especially since, if I'm right about her location, we were both a lot closer to the dangerous area than she was."

Todd stared glumly at the uncooperative CB

133

set. "If the radio worked, I could alert the ski patrol that they need to look for her as well as come to help us out of this."

Cassandra put a hand on his shoulder. "I know," she said kindly. "But why obsess over it? If the set is broken or the signal is jammed, there's nothing you can do about it tonight. And you have no other options for helping her."

"I suppose *you* have a better idea," Todd said.

"As a matter of fact, I do," Cassandra told him. "It's already too dark for them to send out a search party after anyone tonight. So I suggest that we make ourselves comfortable until morning. We could be stuck here for a long time."

Todd nodded. "I suppose you're right."

"So, which will it be?" Cassandra asked. "Would you rather scrounge up a meal for us or get a roaring fire started in the fireplace?"

"Liz says I'm an even worse cook than her sister," he admitted, rolling his eyes. "And believe me, that's bad. But when it comes to fire, I'm a regular pyromaniac."

A slow, lascivious smile spread across Cassandra's face. "That doesn't surprise me," she said, looking him up and down. "You strike me as a guy who knows how to play with fire. You warm things up in here, and I'll get something cooking."

•   •   •

Elizabeth clenched her fists at her side as Dirk walked back across the ski patrol office to his contour map. In one quick motion she zipped up her parka and flipped her hood over her head.

"I can't wait until tomorrow!" she said in a determined voice. "If you won't help me find Todd tonight, I'm going to search for him myself."

She charged out of the office into the deep blue twilight, catching a fleeting glimpse of Dirk's surprised face as she fled. The door banged shut behind her, and the frigid air hit her like a wall.

Elizabeth gasped painfully, unprepared for the biting cold. The wind seemed to whip away every bit of warmth from her body, and every exposed inch of skin seemed to burn. Then a yellow triangle of light split the deep blue-gray blanket of snow at her feet. For a moment her shadow stretched in front of her in the light of the open doorway. Then the snow was dark again.

Suddenly a man's hands were on her shoulders. "Elizabeth!" Dirk yelled. "You can't do this! Come back inside."

"I can't!" she screamed, trying to charge forward against the blast. "I have to find him! I have to!" The wind gusted even more strongly, and Elizabeth had to struggle to keep her footing. Her hood blew back off her forehead. Dirk was right— the weather was just too violent to search for Todd.

She burst into tears, and Dirk turned her around and held her in his arms for a moment as she shook with sobs.

"Come on inside, Elizabeth," he said into her ear. "Please come inside."

Elizabeth nodded and allowed herself to be led back into the ski patrol cabin.

"The tram will be heading back down to the lodge in a half hour," Dirk said gently. "That gives you time for another cup of hot tea to get you warmed up again before you leave here."

"No," she said. "I can't go back down there. Todd managed to get through on the radio once. What if he's still trying to make contact? I have to stay near the radio!"

Dirk nodded. "All right," he agreed. "Normally I wouldn't let you do this. But I doubt you'd pay attention if I told you to go back down to the lodge, so you might as well spend the night here, in case Todd manages to get another message through on the radio. There's a cot in the back office."

In Dirk's hazel eyes, Elizabeth saw not only sympathy but something that looked like approval. She realized that he was impressed by her determination to help Todd. Even in her overwrought state of mind, the knowledge that Dirk thought she had courage sparked a warm glow deep inside her.

"Thanks," Elizabeth said, knowing that she was

thanking him for a lot more than the offer of a cot for the night. "But I'm so worried about Todd that I doubt I'll sleep much. I wonder what he's doing right now. I hope he's not cold and lonely."

Winston tapped on the door to room five-thirteen and waited while Enid fumbled in her backpack for her key.

"Todd and Liz weren't in your room," Enid said. "They weren't in the restaurant. And the slopes are closed early for the night, because of the weather. So they've got to be in here."

"Then why aren't they answering?" Winston asked, knocking harder on the door.

Enid shrugged. "Maybe they were watching television and fell asleep." She pulled out the key and fit it into the lock. Winston followed her in. The room was empty.

"The disco?" Winston suggested.

"I doubt it," Enid said, shaking her head. "They would have waited for us. Besides, it's only seven o'clock—I doubt the disco is even open yet. So where are they? Jessica would say I'm being a mother hen, but Winston, I'm really beginning to get worried."

"You *are* being a mother hen," Winston said. "There are a hundred places where Liz and Todd could be. There's absolutely nothing to be worried—"

Somebody tapped on the door behind them. Winston and Enid spun around to see Mr. Collins in the doorway, his usually smiling face full of concern.

"Good," the handsome English teacher said, "I'm glad we found the two of you together. I already talked to Jessica."

"What's wrong?" Enid asked in a choked voice. "Is it Liz and Todd?"

The teacher motioned for them to sit down on the edge of the bed. "There was an avalanche up near the top of Alpine Peak this evening," he said in a quiet voice.

Winston felt his face go pale. Beside him, Enid went rigid. "Oh, no!" Enid whispered, her green eyes wide. "Were Liz and Todd—"

Mr. Collins put a hand on her shoulder. "It's all right," he said in a soothing voice. "They're fine. We spoke with Elizabeth a little while ago. She's up at the ski patrol station and plans to spend the night there, in case Todd—"

"Where is Todd?" Winston asked, trying to keep his voice steady.

"We're not sure exactly," Mr. Collins admitted. "But Elizabeth and a ski patrol officer spoke to him on a two-way radio. Ms. Jacobi is calling his parents right now, just to alert them to the situation. But we're going to recommend that they stay put for now, since there doesn't seem to be any immediate danger."

"She won't be able to reach them," Winston said. "Todd's parents are in Seattle on business all week."

Mr. Collins nodded and was about to respond, but Enid spoke first. "I don't understand," she said, her voice quavering. "If Liz talked to Todd, then why don't we know where he is?"

"We know he's in a cabin somewhere near the avalanche zone," the teacher said. "We just don't know which one—the radio was cut off before he could tell the patrol his exact location. But the cabin's stocked with supplies, so Todd should be fine until morning, when a search party can reach him. I want you both to relax and try to have a good time this evening. Right now Todd is probably sitting in front of the fireplace with his feet up, enjoying the quiet."

Fires were Todd's forte. He was feeling the pride of a craftsman as he arranged tinder and kindling just so in the stone fireplace. He lit the kindling, and tiny yellow tongues of flame licked the edges of the strategically placed twigs.

Todd felt better already. His head still ached, but the pain was gradually subsiding. And Cassandra was right, he thought, blowing expertly on his growing fire. Elizabeth was probably back at the lodge, perfectly safe—except for being worried sick about *him*. He was the one who was stranded on the mountain. He and Cassandra.

Todd watched the smoke and tiny tendrils of yellow fire creep over to the larger logs, waiting for the exact moment to perform his next operation. He reverently lifted the fireplace poker and turned it in his hand until he had a comfortable grip. Then, like a doctor checking a patient's reflexes, he tapped a smoldering log with the poker in just the right place. The log erupted in a flare of orange flame.

"Hey, that's pretty good!" Cassandra marveled from the table, where she was pouring something gloppy-looking from a can into a cast-iron pot. "You're right. You do have a future as a pyromaniac."

Todd felt absurdly happy at the impressed look on her face. "We'll probably need to keep our ski jackets on for a few more minutes," he said modestly. "It will take a while for this place to warm up."

"Where did you learn to build fires like that?" Cassandra asked. "Do you and your girlfriend go camping a lot?"

"Not much," Todd said. "The last time Liz and I camped together was on a wilderness survival trek in Death Valley."

Cassandra smiled knowingly. "I bet that was romantic. The two of you, out under the stars . . ."

Todd grimaced. "Actually, we were part of a group. And we were so mad at each other that we were barely speaking through a lot of it. Elizabeth got everyone ticked off by telling us all what to do all the time. And I managed to screw up the directions and get everyone lost. Romance was not high on our priority list."

"But I'll bet you had some wonderful, roaring fires while you were there," Cassandra said, carrying the pot over to the fireplace.

"Yes, I guess we did have a few nice ones," Todd said. "I was a much better fire builder than a navigator. Liz, on the other hand, couldn't start a fire if her life depended on it."

Cassandra set down the pot and put her hands on her hips. "Now why doesn't that surprise me?" she asked.

"I still don't know if we should be here," Jessica said to Lila as they sat with Caroline Pearce and Patty Gilbert at the lodge's disco that night. "I mean, it seems wrong for me to be listening to rock music and having a good time while Elizabeth is sleeping in some drafty little ski patrol office at the top of the mountain, waiting for word that Todd has frozen to death."

Lila rolled her eyes. "You exaggerate everything, Jessica. Todd isn't frozen to death. He's in a perfectly safe cabin with plenty of firewood—"

"Except that it's on the wrong side of the mountain and next door to an avalanche," Caroline cheerfully reminded her.

"Well, there is that," Lila conceded.

"Elizabeth was freaking out on the phone," Jessica protested. "She sounded really upset."

"Right," Lila replied. "And I suppose it would make her less upset if she knew that you were moping in your room in sympathy rather than having fun. Even the teachers said we should have fun tonight and try not to worry."

"Well . . . ," Jessica began, slowly stirring her diet soda with her straw.

"You're not making sense, Jess," Lila admonished her. "Look. As dull as Todd is, of course we would be helping out if there were anything at all we could do for him—well, short of actually going outside in the freezing weather and trudging through the snow to look for him," she added.

Patty chuckled, a lock of frizzy black hair falling over her forehead. "You're a real humanitarian, Lila."

"Don't ever say that in public," Lila ordered. "You'd ruin my reputation."

"Lila's right, Jessica," Caroline said. "There really is nothing we can do to help Todd tonight—or to make Elizabeth feel better."

"I guess not," Jessica agreed.

"So why sweat it?" said Lila. "Let's just have a good time, like Mr. Collins and Ms. Jacobi said. Does anyone know how much longer it will be before the band comes back from break?"

"Any minute now," Patty said, checking her watch.

"We're not the only ones who decided to have a good time tonight instead of worrying about Todd and Liz," Caroline said suddenly. "Look over there, at the bar."

Jessica followed Caroline's pointing finger. She nearly choked on her soda. Enid was perched on a stool at the end of the bar, nursing a soda and nervously glancing toward a group of college-age boys.

"Now I've seen everything," Lila announced. "Enid Rollins, sitting alone in a bar, scoping guys."

"Maybe she was abducted by aliens and replaced by an Enid look-alike," Jessica suggested.

"Probably not," Caroline said thoughtfully. Jessica rolled her eyes. Caroline was not known for her sense of humor. "But I bet there's a story here. Maybe I'll just step over there and ask her what's happening. . . ."

"Don't you dare!" Patty protested.

"Why not?" asked Caroline.

"She obviously hasn't seen us," Patty said. "You might embarrass her."

Jessica laughed. "Patty's right," she said. "You wouldn't want to embarrass Enid."

"Since when are you so concerned about Enid's feelings, Jessica?" Lila asked.

"Feelings, schmeelings," Jessica said. She sipped her cola. "All I meant was that if Enid gets

143

all embarrassed and leaves, we'll never find out what she was doing here. If she doesn't know we're in the bar, we can sit here in our dark little corner and watch."

"Very sneaky," Caroline said. "I like that."

"You want to watch Enid Rollins?" Lila asked. "That should be about as exciting as watching the ice melt in my drink."

Jessica shrugged. "Yeah, you're probably right. But if Enid does do something interesting, we'll be right here to see it."

"So what about our plans for tomorrow?" Lila asked, a hopeful tone in her voice. "You're not going to cancel our lesson because of your sister and Todd, are you?"

Jessica frowned. "Maybe we should hang around the lodge in case Elizabeth calls with news."

"Why would you want to do that?" Caroline asked. "I mean, if you're on the mountain all day anyway, you can just take the tram up and see Liz in person anytime you want."

"She's right," Lila said. "But if you want to stay here near the phone all day, I'll understand. I'll let Lu—um, our ski instructor know that you couldn't make it."

Jessica narrowed her eyes at her best friend. "That won't be necessary," she said coldly. She and Lila had called an unspoken truce that evening, after news of the avalanche had reached the lodge. But since it seemed that Todd and Elizabeth were both fine, the war was obviously back on.

Lila smiled. "It really wouldn't be any trouble at all for me to tell him for you," she replied in a voice that would have sounded innocent if Jessica hadn't known better.

"I'm sure it wouldn't trouble you in the least," Jessica said acidly as the band members climbed onto the stage. "But Caroline's right. It's important for me to be on the mountain tomorrow. That way I'll be closer to Elizabeth in case she needs my support."

Lila clenched her jaw. "And closer to somebody else, too," she observed.

With each remark, Jessica noticed, Caroline's head was swinging back and forth from Jessica to Lila, as if she were watching a tennis match.

"Why, whoever could you mean?" Jessica asked, raising her voice to be heard above the opening riffs of a new Jamie Peters song. "Who would I possibly want to get close to at a time like this, except my own twin sister?"

"You know very well who I mean," Lila said. "But it won't make any difference! Face it, Jessica, you don't stand a chance. With my new ski suit—"

"Would someone tell me what we're talking

about here?" Caroline interjected, holding up her hands in a time-out signal.

"Not me," Patty said with a laugh. "This sounds like a Jess-and-Lila war. I've seen them before, and it's too easy for innocent bystanders to get caught in the cross fire."

"Oh, I don't know," Caroline said. "I think it's pretty exciting."

"I can think of something much more exciting," Patty said, her dark, pretty face lighting up. "See that guy who's heading this way—the one who looks like Denzel Washington? He's been watching us for the last ten minutes. I think he's about to ask me to dance."

Jessica looked up, surprised. She'd been so intent on worrying about Elizabeth and then fighting with Lila that she'd forgotten her favorite spectator sport—scoping guys. "You know, Patty, I think you're right," she said. "I wonder if he has a friend."

"Bon appetit!" Cassandra called, placing the cast-iron pot on the table.

Todd was so hungry he'd have eaten his ski bindings. But Cassandra's creation actually smelled great—warm and savory and filling.

"I can't believe you whipped this up out of a few old cans of soup and stuff," Todd said. "I'm glad one of us can cook."

"Don't say that until you taste it," Cassandra warned as Todd dished some up. "I'm not even sure what it is, really," she admitted. "It's sort of a stew thing, I guess. I mixed two different kinds of canned soup with a can of garbanzo beans and threw some stale cracker crumbs over the top. There wasn't a whole lot to work with. Is it any good?"

Todd nodded, his mouth too full to reply.

"Does your girlfriend cook?" Cassandra asked. "Is she into the whole domestic thing?"

"Well, I wouldn't call her Suzy Homemaker," Todd said. "I mean, Elizabeth is pretty career-oriented. But she cooks for her family a lot of the time, and she does a good job of it. Liz and her sister are supposed to take turns," he added, "but Jessica usually manages to coerce Liz into doing it for her, too."

"Ah," Cassandra said. "So she's a real pushover, huh?" She winked. "I guess that's a good trait to find in a girlfriend if you're a healthy, normal teenage boy."

Todd felt his face coloring. He shoved another spoonful of the stew into his mouth and gulped it down. "N-n-no, I wouldn't call Liz a pushover at all," he stammered. "I mean, Jessica's the only one who can get away with that stuff. With anyone else, Liz is sensitive and thoughtful—but she's also a strong-minded person who knows what she wants."

147

He'd always liked that about Elizabeth. But when he said it to Cassandra, it sounded like a character flaw.

Cassandra twirled her spoon in her bowl of stew. For some reason, it was an incredibly seductive gesture. "I bet I know what Liz wants tonight," she said in her throaty voice. "She must be missing you plenty—all by her lonesome in your room at the lodge, without her roommate to keep her warm."

Todd's eyes flew open wider. "No!" he gasped. "I mean, Elizabeth *does* have her roommate with her. She's sharing a room with her best friend, Enid. It's *my* roommate, Winston, who's all alone tonight." Mentally he wished Winston a good night's sleep on a real bed.

"I swear, Todd," Cassandra said, "you strike me as a guy who's in desperate need of a real woman. If I were sixteen years old and had a boyfriend who looked like you, Winston would be sleeping downstairs in the lobby in about three seconds flat."

Cassandra was obviously someone who would appreciate the beauty and purpose of his DO NOT DISTURB sign, Todd realized. There was no doubt about it now: Cassandra really was coming onto him. He was intrigued but terrified. He didn't know if he should thank his lucky stars—or flee outside to sleep under them.

What do I do now? he asked himself. What

would any guy in his position do if a beautiful woman threw herself at him?

It depends on the guy, Todd decided, his mind racing. Kirk "the Jerk" Anderson would exchange a few raunchy comments with Cassandra and then help her out of her ski suit. Bruce Patman, the richest boy in Sweet Valley, would pull out a cellular phone and call a helicopter to whisk the two of them off to a private condo in Aspen.

Winston would probably just faint.

But what about Todd "Whizzer" Wilkins, high-school basketball star and devoted—but frustrated—boyfriend of Elizabeth Wakefield? What would he do in this situation?

Regretfully, he knew what the answer had to be. "Uh, speaking of beds," he said, looking at his bowl, "why don't you take the cot, Cassandra? I'll sleep on that couch in the corner."

Elizabeth rode alone in the big red car of the aerial tram. But there was no glass in the windows, and the freezing wind chilled her to her core. It was dusk, and the blanket of snow on the mountainside below was a deep blue-gray. The car lurched over a coupling in the cable. Elizabeth gasped. A rumble like thunder shook the tram, and she was tumbling in slow motion down a tremendous distance, through blue twilight.

Then she was face down in the cold, wet snow, shaking with fear. She heard skis whirring. Todd was gliding toward her in his hunter green coat. Elizabeth saw him and felt safe.

"Look!" Todd called. "The moon is coming up." Its silver crescent hung between two inky black peaks.

But the wind blew harder, and the cottony flakes of snow turned to whirling stars. "Todd?" Elizabeth called uncertainly. He kept skiing toward her, but the distance between them was growing, and Elizabeth didn't know why.

A loud roar shattered the day, and the ground shifted. A mountain of snow and ice was rushing toward Todd with the force of a runaway freight train.

Elizabeth's limbs were frozen to the ground. "Todd!" she screamed. The avalanche washed over him like an ocean wave. When the rumbling stopped, the mountainside lay still and empty, except for the tops of pine trees, their boughs etched in crystal.

Elizabeth broke off a branch and tore into the blue-tinged snow. She dug frantically, panting with the effort. The hunter green of Todd's parka showed hazily beneath the ice. But it kept moving deeper into the mountain, more distant from Elizabeth's desperate hands.

Elizabeth sat straight up in the cot in Dirk's office. She was shivering, but sweat poured down her face. "Todd!" she whispered to the empty room. "Where are you?" A terrible longing washed over her, and hot tears spilled from her eyes. Wherever Todd might be, she guessed that he was cold and frightened and lonely. And she wished she could be there to comfort him and to fall asleep, just once, in his arms.

Todd shifted his body uncomfortably on the lumpy couch in the ski cabin. He suddenly had a much greater appreciation for Winston's unnecessary sacrifice of the night before. His muscles were still sore from his wipeout in the avalanche. And the too-short couch didn't help. If he stretched his aching legs, they hung over the side of the armrest, cutting off the circulation in his feet and leaving his toes hanging out in the cold. But when he scrunched his legs up, his knees hung off the edge of the cushion.

The room was tinged with the orange glow of embers in the fireplace, and he could just make out the bed across the cabin, where Cassandra lay. He'd seen her peeling off her scarlet ski suit before getting into bed. It had been hard not to see, in such a small cabin. Especially when she so obviously wanted him to. Underneath, she wore a two-piece set of silk long underwear that hugged her body even more closely than the formfitting ski suit.

Todd pushed Cassandra out of his mind. He

had to sleep. He would need every bit of brainpower the next day if they were to find a way back to the lodge. He needed his rest.

He burrowed under the scratchy wool blanket. The cabin was getting colder, and the blanket turned to snow. He was trapped beneath it, beneath tons of ice and snow. He knew he would freeze to death, but he was too tired to care. At least he would get some sleep.

Suddenly he was warm. Elizabeth was with him, her hand caressing his shoulder, her lips brushing against his. His pulse began to race with life. He pulled her close and kissed her tenderly. "Elizabeth," he breathed.

A throaty laugh confused him, and his eyes flew open. "Cassandra!" he cried, sitting up so quickly that he nearly knocked her off the edge of the couch. The top part of her long underwear had been pushed up slightly, and a narrow crescent of creamy skin showed at her waist. Todd wrenched his eyes away from her. "What do you think you're doing?"

Cassandra laughed again. "If you don't know, then you need a real woman even more desperately than I thought!"

"Cassandra, I told you that I have a girlfriend," Todd reminded her. "*Elizabeth* is my girlfriend! Remember?"

Cassandra waved her hand. "So? What does that have to do with us?"

"There is no *us!*" Todd protested. He wished that Mr. Collins would appear in the doorway and order Cassandra back to her bed. "I'm in love with Elizabeth!" Todd insisted, his head throbbing again.

Cassandra rolled her eyes. "If only my second ex-husband had been this faithful," she mused.

Todd gulped. "*Second* ex-husband?" he asked.

"Well, Toddy boy," Cassandra purred, "if you change your mind, you know where to find me." She sighed a deep, throaty sigh, and Todd felt his face growing warm. "I just don't understand this younger generation," Cassandra concluded.

She yawned, stretching her sinuous arms over her head in a fluid motion that reminded Todd of a panther. Then she glided across the room to the bed. Todd tried not to watch her, but his eyes followed her white-suited figure as she slid beneath the blanket.

He lay back on the lumpy couch and stared at the ceiling, waiting for dawn.

Chapter 9

Elizabeth half-woke from a restless sleep to hear voices in the next room. For a moment she thought she was in her own bed back in Sweet Valley, listening to the sounds of her family starting the day. Then she recognized Dirk's tenor drawl. Her eyes flew open. She was in the back room of the ski patrol office, and Todd had been caught in an avalanche. She realized that the search parties must be preparing to leave.

"Good morning, Liz," Dirk said as she emerged into the main office. "I'd like to ask how you slept," he said, a kind look on his handsome face, "but I expect I know the answer."

"I'm OK," Elizabeth said with a shrug. "The radio was quiet all night."

"I thought so," Dirk replied. "Look, we've

154

got things under control here. Why don't you catch the tram back down to the lodge? We'll radio the main ski patrol office there as soon as there's any news."

"What if Todd radios here?" Elizabeth asked.

"I'm leaving one person in the office to monitor the radio and coordinate between the search parties," Dirk explained.

"Then let me come with you!" Elizabeth pleaded suddenly. "I want to help find Todd."

"You're a very brave young woman," Dirk said. "But this is specialized work, Liz. These people are professionals." He smiled. "Don't worry. We know what we're doing. We'll find him."

"You'll be out there yourself?" Elizabeth asked.

"I'm leading one of the search parties," Dirk said. "And Donna will lead the other."

For some reason, Elizabeth felt better that Dirk would be out there personally, looking for Todd. Dirk was someone she trusted instinctively. "OK," she said. "But I don't think I'll take the tram down the mountain. I want to ski instead. Maybe the exercise will take my mind off things."

"Good idea," Dirk said.

"First I need to get a message to my friends and teachers down there," she said. "They must be worried sick."

*　　　*　　　*

Enid scanned the message that had been called in to the front desk of the lodge while she and Winston were at breakfast. "Elizabeth is OK," she told Winston. "The search parties have just headed out to look for Todd, and she's on her way down the mountain. She says to wait for her by the skating pond in front of the lodge. Do you want to head that way now?"

"We've got time," Winston reminded her. "It will take Liz a while to ski down the whole mountain."

"I know, but where else do we have to go?" Enid pointed out.

Winston nodded, and they began walking toward the skating pond. "How are, uh, *things*?" Winston asked.

Enid rolled her eyes. Since the day before, she and Winston had been skirting the issue of *101 Ways to Be Sassy*—just as they'd avoided speaking directly about Winston's klutziness on the slopes. But she was feeling too drained and hopeless for subterfuge. Winston was one of her best friends. Maybe he could help.

"I suppose you're talking about my new book," she replied after a thoughtful pause. She was grateful that the skating pond area was deserted this early in the morning. "Well, things could be better," she admitted. "I took your advice and went out last night, despite what was happening with

Todd and Liz. But I bombed out, as usual. It's pathetic. I can sit in the middle of a bar full of guys, and I still can't get a single one interested in me. So much for Method Five."

Winston blushed. Enid knew it was a difficult subject for him to be serious about, but he was trying to help. He leaned on the split-log railing and looked out over the frozen pond. "You're pretty shy with strangers, Enid," he said gently. "Are you sure you let them know that *you* were interested in them?"

"Three times I asked guys to dance," Enid said. "How much more interested could I be? Every one of them fled back to the bar as soon as the music stopped."

"Maybe the kind of guy who hangs out in bars just isn't your type," Winston suggested.

"You got that right," Enid said. She bit her lip thoughtfully. "You know, you're a guy, Winston."

Winston's eyes widened. "I've heard that," he said.

Enid smiled. "Tell me honestly. What's wrong with me? I know I'm not gorgeous like Liz, or vivacious like Jessica, or elegant like Lila. But there has to be something else!"

"There's nothing wrong with you, Enid. If it hadn't been for Maria, I'd have been interested myself on the slopes yesterday—until I saw it was you." He blushed. "That didn't come out exactly right," he admitted.

Enid laughed, strangely cheered by his awkwardness. "That's OK, Winston. I think I know what you mean. I, um, kind of felt the same way."

They stared at each other for a moment, and Enid felt her own face coloring to match his. Then they both jerked their gazes away, to the skating pond.

"So what's next?" Winston asked.

Enid stared thoughtfully at the smooth, thick ice. "Ice skating," she said.

"I meant with your hundred and one ways," Winston said.

"So did I," she said. "Actually, I have several next steps. I still have to wear the cool shades I bought." She patted the pocket where the new, high-tech goggles were waiting. "That's Method Four. And then I have to find a way to let guys know I'm a sports fan—Method Six. But I noticed ice skating a few pages ahead in the book—I think it's Method Twelve. Supposedly guys like skating with a girl. It's like dancing, but it makes them feel more macho, because they can keep her from falling and hurting herself—which is even more true in my case, since I'm as rotten at ice skating as I am at picking up guys in bars."

"Can you try two methods at once?" Winston asked.

"Skating while picking up guys in bars?" Enid asked, mystified.

"No," said Winston. "Skating while wearing spiffy lenses. There's a bunch of people headed toward the rink. And most of them are male. Slip on those cool shades of yours, and let's see what happens."

"But I don't have any ice skates with me!" Enid protested.

"You can rent them at that little stand over there," Winston said, pointing. "You might as well," he said when Enid opened her mouth to object. "We've got to do *something* while we wait for Liz."

A few minutes later Winston stood a few paces from the pond, studiously staring away from Enid so that nobody would know they were together. Enid, wobbling on her rented skates, grasped the railing with one hand while she slipped on the neon purple ski goggles with the other. Luckily, the sun had just broken through a bank of low clouds, and the morning was suddenly bright enough so that she didn't feel ridiculous in dark lenses.

Enid hated acting the role of a helpless woman. But on ice skates she had no choice. She pushed forward one foot and then the other while pulling hand over hand on the railing to propel herself around the edge of the pond.

"You look like you could use some help," said a deep voice behind her. Enid nearly fell over in her scramble to turn toward its owner. She almost gasped aloud. The goggles were so dark that it was hard to see clearly. But she was looking into the face of a tall, dark-haired skater with chiseled features, a lean, powerful body, and twinkling eyes. Enid felt hope rising in her chest.

Then it thudded to her feet. Next to the handsome male skater was a pretty blonde in a short skating skirt. "Maybe we could give you a few pointers," the girl said, smiling.

"Uh, no, thanks," Enid said with a weak laugh. "I'm sure I'll figure it out as I go along."

The attractive couple skated off. Enid flashed Winston a weak grin to show him she wasn't discouraged. He gave her a thumbs-up signal, and she turned her concentration back to keeping the blades of her skates on the ice.

"Come on, purple goggles," she whispered. "Do your magic."

"Nifty shades!" said another male voice, as if in answer to her prayer. Then her feet nearly flew out from under her, and Enid gripped the railing as if it were a lifeline. The Green Ponytail Dude was skating toward her, flannel shirt flapping as his nose ring glinted in the morning sunlight. "But I miss the green nose color you were wearing yesterday," he continued. Enid flinched when he took her arm. "That was a truly awesome nose color."

Enid smiled weakly, throwing Winston a get-me-out-of-this glance over the Green Ponytail Dude's shoulder.

"I guess I, like, left the nose color in my room this morning," Enid apologized.

"Bummer," he replied, his head bouncing up and down. "You wanna, like, skate or something?" he asked. "I've invented a new technique. I call it slam-skating."

"Enid!" Winston called, reaching over the railing toward her.

"Sorry," Enid whispered to the Green Ponytail Dude. "That's my boyfriend, Winston, and he can be pretty violent when he's jealous."

"Oh," said the boy, dropping her arm as if it were on fire. "Bummer." He edged away quickly and then dashed off across the ice.

"Maybe it's time for Method Six," Winston suggested. "Trade caps with me," he said, pulling off his knit cap and handing it to her. Enid looked curiously at the purple-and-black cap in her hand. "A Colorado Rockies hat?" she asked.

"I picked it up at the gift shop at the rest stop on the way here," Winston explained. "Why don't you borrow it for a couple of days? Maybe it will bring you luck."

Enid nodded gratefully. "I'm ditching the shades, too," she said, pulling them off and stuffing them back into her pocket. "Besides attracting the wrong guys, they're so dark I can hardly see where I'm going." She blinked in the bright sunshine. Then she noticed a figure in navy blue walking toward them from the lodge. "There's Elizabeth!" she yelled. "Help me get these skates off!"

"There's Lucas!" Jessica said excitedly, shouldering her skis and elbowing Lila out of the way so that she could reach the ski instructor first. He was so tall that she could glimpse his dark head above the crowd of skiers waiting near the main chairlift.

"You don't have to push," Lila complained as they hurried toward Lucas. "It doesn't make any difference if you get to him a split second before I do. No matter how hard you try to prevent it, I'm the one who's going to get the first kiss from Lucas King. I mean, face it, Jess. How can he resist?"

The girls reached Lucas and stopped short. A pretty, petite girl was standing with him, balancing on her ski poles. She had very short dark hair and wore a trim black ski suit with a stylish but totally impractical red tam on her head.

"This is Karen Newman," Lucas said, pointing to the girl. "Jessica Wakefield and Lila Fowler," he added, continuing his introductions. "Karen will be joining our lesson today, if you two don't mind. She's a beginner and needs some personal attention."

Karen was standing still. But as if on cue, she

immediately slipped and fell to the ground.

"Oops," Karen said with a giggle.

Jessica groaned. This girl *really* didn't know how to ski.

"The search parties are out looking," Elizabeth informed Enid and Winston as the three began walking back toward the lodge. She laughed bitterly. "Search *party*," she mused. "What a stupid name for it. Some party."

Winston's face grew thoughtful, and he opened his mouth as if to say something. But he was interrupted by Mr. Collins, who hurried up to them, wearing ski clothes, and fell into step.

"Elizabeth, are you all right?" he asked his star pupil.

Elizabeth tried to look cheerful. "I'm fine," she told her favorite teacher, knowing that he wasn't fooled for a minute. In addition to being her English teacher, Mr. Collins was the faculty sponsor for the student newspaper at Sweet Valley High, as well as a friend and confidante of Elizabeth and the rest of the newspaper staff.

"No word on Todd yet?" Mr. Collins asked in a sympathetic voice.

Elizabeth shook her head.

"It's been a while since you left the station at the summit," Enid said. "Maybe we should call up there and see if there's any news."

"As soon as I made it down the mountain, I stopped by the main ski patrol station, behind the lodge," Elizabeth said. "Dirk hadn't checked in yet."

"Dirk?" Mr. Collins asked.

Elizabeth shrugged. "He's the ski patrol guy who's heading up the search effort," she said. "He really helped me out last night." She blinked back tears at the memory of her long, horrible night on the mountain.

"Don't worry, Liz," Winston said. "Todd is fine. I bet they'll find him within the next few hours, and we can all be toasting marshmallows in the fireplace by evening."

"Winston's right," Enid said staunchly. "You said you heard his voice over the radio last night. He said he's OK."

"I know, but I can't stop thinking of him, cold and hungry. He could be injured, for all we know!"

"Nah," Winston said. "Todd's too good a skier for that. But I bet you're right about one thing— he's going to be pretty hungry when he gets back. So I suggest we keep busy by planning the biggest, best welcome-back party this place has ever seen."

"That's not a bad idea, Winston," Mr. Collins said.

Winston grinned almost convincingly. "Let's show these Colorado folks that Californians are still the masters when it comes to partying!"

164

"Thanks for trying to cheer me up, Winston," Elizabeth said, "but I'm not really in the mood for a party."

"That doesn't matter," Winston said. "The party isn't for you, anyway. It's for Todd. And Todd is always in the mood for a party."

"Come on, Liz!" Enid urged. "It'll be fun!"

"And it may help get your mind off all the worst-case scenarios," Mr. Collins pointed out.

Elizabeth nodded. "OK," she agreed. "Let's throw a party." On one level, she knew that her friends were right. Todd was probably in perfect health, sitting in a boring but safe cabin on the east ridge of Alpine Peak. But in her mind, the last scene of her nightmare played out in slow motion. Despite the happy cries of skiers and skaters that filled the air, Elizabeth heard nothing but the eerie silence after the avalanche. And all she could see was the image of Todd's hunter green parka far below the surface of the deadly ice.

Todd paced from one end of the cabin to the other. "What time is it?" he asked Cassandra. His own watch had been broken when he wiped out in the avalanche.

"Five minutes after the last time you asked," Cassandra said in a relaxed, slightly amused tone.

She stretched languorously on the couch. "Eleven in the morning," she added.

"Why are they taking so long?" Todd asked. "The ski patrol has to know we're out here. I'm sure somebody heard my call last night. So why isn't a rescue party here?"

Cassandra turned over on the couch, arching her back like a cat. "That was a pretty hefty pile of snow that got dumped outside the doorstep here," she reminded him. "It could be days before anyone can dig through it to get to us."

Todd whirled. "Days?" he yelled. "I can't stay here for days!"

Cassandra breathed a throaty sigh. "My company isn't all that unappealing, is it?"

"No!" Todd said, too quickly. "I mean, it's not that. I mean—"

"Relax, Todd," she told him, rising slowly and easily. "We can manage here for a few days, just the two of us." As she spoke she glided toward him. "In fact, it could be rather fun—we'll be like two soul mates who discover each other . . . stranded on a desert island . . ."

Todd stopped in his tracks. Cassandra was very close to him now—close enough for him to feel uncomfortable—but he couldn't bring himself to move away. Slowly and carefully, Cassandra leaned in and kissed him lightly on the cheek.

Of its own volition, Todd's hand rose to his cheek. His heart was pounding so hard he could feel the blood throbbing in his temples. Cassandra gazed steadily into his eyes. The cabin was chilly, but Todd felt sweat prickling along the back of his neck.

"No strings attached," Cassandra breathed, caressing the side of his face with her cool, smooth hand.

"I-I-I think we're running low on firewood," Todd stammered. "If we're going to be here a while, I should head outside and see if I can find any."

Despite the cold temperature, Lila was steamed. "I'm paying good money for these lessons," she said to Jessica as they watched Lucas correct Karen's form for the hundredth time that morning. "And now that little twerp is taking up all of Lucas's time. I want some hands-on training!"

And hands-on training, she decided, *is exactly what I'm going to get.* It was time for some decisive action.

Before Jessica could respond, Lila skied over to Lucas and managed to position herself between him and Karen. "I'm still having trouble with the traversing movement," she told Lucas, trusting her new white-and-silver snowsuit to work its magic on him. "I think I'd understand it better if you'd ski across the mountain with me, with your hands on my hips."

Out of the corner of her eye, Lila saw Jessica clench her jaw.

"It looks to me like you've got that movement down perfectly," Lucas replied.

"No, I don't," Lila said quickly. "Trust me. It may look right, but it doesn't *feel* right. I just know I'm doing something wrong."

Lucas shrugged. "You're the boss," he said. Then he turned to Jessica. "Jess, would you do me a big favor?"

Jessica smiled flirtatiously. "Anything, Lucas," she promised.

"While I'm working with Lila, would you help Karen with her stops?"

Jessica's smile froze, so that she looked as if she were trying to swallow a baseball whole. "I'd be happy to," she said in a very low voice. Only Lila knew her well enough to realize how angry Jessica was.

"It serves her right," Lila said under her breath a minute later as she skied away with Lucas's strong, warm hands on her hips.

"You're doing fine, Lila," Lucas told her a few minutes later. "I told you that you didn't need any special instruction. All you need is a little confidence."

Inwardly Lila smirked. Confidence was not a problem. All she really needed was for Jessica— and Karen—to be carried off by caribou.

"See?" Lucas said. "You've got it down pat. I think we can head back to Jess and Karen now."

Lila promptly stumbled, allowing Lucas to grab her so she wouldn't fall. "No, I'm still not completely sure," she said, turning around to face him. "But I know I do it much better when you're holding me." She looked up into his eyes, and his gaze locked on hers. Lila's face grew warm. *This is it,* she told herself. It was time for Lila to win the bet. *Eat your heart out, Jessica!* she thought, parting her lips slightly to meet his.

"Yo, Lucas!" a voice called. A red-haired, athletic-looking guy skied expertly to a stop beside them, showering Lila with snow. She quickly extracted herself from Lucas's arms. "Will you be at the party tonight?" the young man asked Lucas. Lila saw that he wore an instructor's badge like Lucas's.

"Hey, Scott!" Lucas greeted him. "Is the party at Ann's apartment, like always?"

"No," said Scott. "We've moved it to Marge's place—it's on Brighton Court, the last house on the cul-de-sac. Things will be heating up around nine thirty."

Lucas flashed him a smile. "I'll be there!" he called as Scott skied away.

"So will I," Lila muttered under her breath. "Count on it."

◦   ◦   ◦

"Oops!" Jessica said a few hours later as she walked back toward the ski lodge with Lila and Karen to buy more lip balm. "I still had some lip balm left all along! I guess I was looking in the wrong pocket before. Well, you two go ahead, and I'll just wait back there with Lucas."

She flashed Lila a triumphant smile and turned to scurry back to Lucas. She had done it. She'd tricked Lila into giving her a few minutes alone with the instructor.

"Lucas?" she asked him a few minutes later, after she'd strapped her skis back on. "I don't quite have the positioning down for the parallel skiing you were showing me. Could you show me *exactly* how to position my body?"

"Sure, Jess," Lucas said. "Just watch me and do exactly as I do."

Jessica pretended to try. "You know, I can't seem to get it right. Am I holding my shoulders too far forward or too far back?"

Lucas stepped closer and placed his hands on her left shoulder. "Rotate it like this—" he began. Suddenly he fell against Jessica, hard, and they both collapsed in the snow. A moment later, Karen was rolling off them.

"Sorry, guys!" Karen said, her unnatural perkiness slowly driving Jessica insane. "I guess I still need to work on those stops."

Jessica rolled over in the snow, so frustrated that she was almost ready to give up. At this rate, she would never even get Lucas alone for five minutes, let alone get him to kiss her. As gorgeous as he was, she just wasn't sure anymore if he was worth the trouble.

As she scrambled to her feet, she saw Lila reaching out a hand to help Lucas up. She held on to his hand a lot longer than necessary, Jessica thought. And the way she was standing with her hip jutting out—it was so *obvious*. "Are you all right?" Lila was asking Lucas in her most sugary tone.

Jessica shook her head, her resolve strengthened. She couldn't let Lila win. She just couldn't.

Chapter 10

Elizabeth jumped when she felt a hand on her shoulder.

"Sorry, Liz," Jessica said, sitting next to her on the window seat of the hotel's lounge. "I didn't mean to startle you. But you looked like you could use some cheering up."

Elizabeth shook her head. "I don't want to be cheered up," she said. "I want Todd."

"I know," Jessica said with a sigh. "It would be a much livelier welcome-back party if the guest of honor had been able to make it."

Elizabeth kicked at a balloon that was beginning to look shriveled. "I guess we should have canceled the party," she said.

"Maybe," Jessica said with a shrug. "But Winston figured that the pizzas had already been ordered,

172

and as Mr. Collins said, we all had to eat anyway—"

"That was only an excuse," Elizabeth interrupted. "I know Winston and Mr. Collins. They just wanted to help us get our minds off Todd—especially me."

"It isn't working very well, is it?" Jessica asked.

"I keep looking out this window toward the mountain, expecting to see Todd walking down the path from the tram at any minute," Elizabeth said, her eyes misting over. "But he doesn't come! Jessica, it's been more than twenty-four hours!"

Somewhere behind the twins, Winston was trying to fan enthusiasm for a halfhearted game of charades.

"Winston can be a real jerk," Jessica said grumpily.

"No, he isn't," Elizabeth defended her friend automatically. "He and Todd are very close. Winston's just trying to keep busy so he doesn't think too much."

"There's not much danger of that," Jessica commented, rolling her eyes.

"Maybe the ski patrol has left a message for me since the last time I checked," Elizabeth said hopefully. "Hand me that courtesy phone." She dialed the hotel operator. "Is this the front desk? This is Elizabeth Wakefield, room five-thirteen. Are there any messages for me?"

"No," said the now-familiar voice of the bored woman on the other end of the line. "Not in the last five minutes."

Elizabeth slammed down the phone, tears spilling out of her eyes. "I can't do this anymore!" she cried, jumping up from the window seat. "I've got to be up on Alpine Peak, near the radio!"

"Liz, it's dark and cold out there!" Jessica objected. "The ski patrol guy will call you if he hears anything from Todd."

Elizabeth shook her head. "No, I have to be up there myself, closer to where the searchers are. I'm going to take the tram back up the mountain and spend the night in the ski patrol office."

"Mr. Collins and Ms. Jacobi will have a hissy fit!"

"Not if you don't tell them," Elizabeth said, feeling a twinge of remorse at keeping the chaperones in the dark. But she knew Jessica would keep her secret. Jessica was the last person to worry about following the rules.

"Do you want me to come with you?" Jessica offered.

"No," Elizabeth said slowly. "You stay here and try to have a good time, if you can. With this group, Winston needs all the help he can get."

Caroline was pantomiming something that involved flapping her arms like a bird and sticking her nose in the air while her classmates called out inane guesses. Lila rolled her eyes. She loathed charades. She checked her watch. It was quarter to nine, about time for her to slip away from Jessica and the others.

Jessica, she noted, was standing near the window with Elizabeth, who seemed agitated. *Good*, Lila thought. As long as Jessica was distracted by Elizabeth's mood, she would be too busy to keep tabs on Lila.

Lila stopped a hotel employee and asked, "Excuse me, where is the nearest rest room?" pitching her voice just loud enough to be sure her friends overheard. She pulled a lipstick from her purse and walked toward the rest room as if to freshen her makeup. But instead she rounded the corner and hurried toward her own room to change into her black leather jeans and sparkling silver blouse.

She had a real party to get to.

"My party was a bust," Winston said in a discouraged tone. "I think that's the first time I ever planned one that started breaking up by nine thirty." He and Enid were collecting the empty pizza boxes while Jessica popped the remaining balloons.

Enid smiled sympathetically. "It wasn't your

fault, Winston," she said. "Welcome-back parties are a lot more fun when the person being welcomed is present."

"Elizabeth left early," Winston said. "I hope she's not upstairs in your room, alone and miserable."

Jessica popped a limp-looking pink balloon. "She's not," she said. "She's up on the mountain in the ski patrol office, alone and miserable."

"What?" Enid asked. "You let her go back up there to spend another night all by herself on the top of the mountain?"

"Don't blame me!" Jessica protested. "I tried to talk her out of it. I even tried to go with her. She wouldn't listen."

"So what about Lila?" Enid asked. "Why did she leave early? She didn't seem terribly broken up about Todd. But I haven't seen her in more than half an hour."

Jessica froze. "No," she began in a low, tense voice. "She couldn't have—" She bolted out of the room, leaving Enid and Winston staring after her.

"What was that all about?" Enid asked.

"It's too late for a shopping trip," Winston said. "With Jess and Lila, that leaves only one thing—"

"A guy," Enid completed for him. "Yes, you're probably right. As Elizabeth said the other night, sometimes with Jessica it's safer not to know the details."

"Speaking of guys," Winston said, "did you have any luck in the love-life department today? Did my Colorado Rockies cap sweep some sports fan off his feet?"

Enid laughed. "Oh, it worked, all right. But I figured out what kind of guys like girls who wear team logos—guys who can't talk about anything but sports!"

"Bummer," Winston said sympathetically, imitating the Green Ponytail Dude.

Enid laughed. "Then I tried skiing in non-ski clothes—jeans and lots of sweaters," she continued. "The book said it was a good way to attract boys who are nonconformists. All I attracted was frostbite. I told jokes in the lift line, and nobody laughed. I even 'accidentally' mixed up my own skis with the pair that belonged to this tall blond guy from the East Coast. He was very nice about it. He was also gay."

"Oh," Winston said.

"In all honesty, I probably wasn't giving it a fair shot today," Enid admitted. "I kept thinking about Todd and about what Liz is going through. I guess I wasn't feeling very sassy."

"I haven't been the life of the party myself," Winston said.

"But Elizabeth keeps insisting that we should get out on the slopes instead of moping around about Todd," Enid said. "Maybe we'll feel better about things tomorrow."

"So which number are you up to in the book?" Winston asked.

"Next comes Method Eighteen—snowboarding."

Winston nodded. "Sounds like a good way to pick up an orthopedic surgeon."

"Do you think I need to make out a last will and testament?" Enid asked.

"That depends," Winston said. "Are you leaving anything to me?"

"I already gave you my lime green zinc oxide," Enid reminded him. "Some people are never satisfied."

Jessica threw open the door of her room. Sure enough, it was empty—and Lila's coat and purse were gone.

"Rats!" she yelled, pounding one fist into her palm. Lila was up to something, and Jessica was one hundred percent certain that it had something to do with Lucas. "Where can that rich little fink be?"

Through the open door of the bathroom, Jessica spotted something red. She stepped closer and saw a message scrawled in lipstick on the mirror, in Lila's handwriting: *Gotcha!*

Elizabeth sat at the desk in the ski patrol office

just before ten o'clock Monday night, staring at the radio as if it were a television. The officer who had been monitoring the set all day had just left, and Dirk was expected back at any moment.

"Please contact me, Todd," she begged aloud. "Please get through!"

The door banged open and a freezing gust of wind buffeted the room. Dirk struggled to close the door behind him. Then he staggered across the room and collapsed on the couch. Elizabeth poured him a cup of tea.

"What is it?" she asked. "Did you find him?"

Dirk shook his head. There was ice in his hair, and he was breathing too heavily to talk.

He drank the scalding tea in one gulp. "It's worse than we thought out there," he told her finally. He began fumbling with the snaps on his parka, but his fingers were obviously too numb. Elizabeth gently pushed his hands out of the way and helped him out of the wet jacket.

"Did you see where the avalanche was?" she asked.

Dirk shook his head. "We couldn't even get near it," he admitted, his voice hoarse. "That whole ridge is too unstable. There could be another avalanche at any minute."

Elizabeth choked back a sob. Even if Todd was warm and safe in a well-stocked cabin, he could still be in terrible danger.

"But you know where the cabins are," Elizabeth said. "Can't you just go to every one of them until you find Todd?"

Dirk shook his head. "Most of them are completely cut off," he said. "The avalanche was a huge one, from all indications. We tried to approach it from three different angles, but the whole ridge is impassable."

"But Todd might be injured!" Elizabeth cried. "You have to get to him before it's too late!" At Dirk's stricken look, she instantly regretted her words. "I'm sorry," she said in a quiet voice. "I know you're doing everything you can."

Her eyes met his, and Dirk took her warm hand in his cold one. "Not quite," he said. "I've already called for a rescue helicopter for tomorrow morning—if the weather conditions are good enough to try it. It's the only way we can reach that part of the mountain."

Elizabeth nodded. "I'm coming with you," she stated simply.

"I'm sorry, Elizabeth," Dirk told her. "But I can't allow that."

"I'm coming with you," she repeated. "Or I'm going in by myself, on skis."

Dirk stared at her steadily, as if he was sizing up her resolve. "All right," he said finally in his soft drawl. "It's against the rules—and your chaperones

180

would have my head if they knew I was allowing it. But you can join the rescue mission tomorrow."

As the cab pulled away, Lila stamped her feet outside the door of the last house on Brighton Court. From inside, she could hear the sounds of a party in full swing. She rang the bell again, but nobody answered. Finally she shrugged and pushed open the door.

"Hi there!" called a young woman who looked like a model. Lila could barely hear her over the din. The woman gestured with a cup of what smelled like mulled cider. "I'm Marge," she said. "You must be one of the new ski instructors."

"Uh, yeah," Lila said. "That's right. I'm a friend of Lucas King. Is he here?"

Marge nodded across the room, and Lila saw Lucas standing near the fireplace with his friend Scott. She smiled her thanks to Marge. Then she pushed through the crowded room toward Lucas, unzipping her parka to give him the full benefit of her dazzling silver blouse.

Tonight is the night, Lila thought. She could feel it in her bones. She would have hours to spend with Lucas, and Jessica had no way of finding them. She could almost feel his lips on hers.

"Game, set, and match to the girl in the silver blouse," Lila whispered under her breath. She couldn't wait to see the look on Jessica's face when she found out.

Static jangled over the radio, drowning out the howl of the snowstorm that raged outside that night near the top of the mountain. Todd turned the knob. "Please come in!" he called into the microphone for what seemed like the thousandth time. "We've been stranded by the avalanche, in a cabin on the east face of Alpine Peak. Send help!"

Cassandra rested a hand on his shoulder. "Todd, you've been trying for hours," she said. Her hand began caressing and then kneading his sore, tense muscles. "It's no use wearing yourself out like this," she said. "Nobody can hear you."

"But this is our best chance to get through," he said, rubbing his burning eyes. Now Cassandra was kneading his shoulders with both hands. The contact unnerved him, especially after the incident the night before. At the same time, he realized as he slowly rolled his head forward, he really didn't want her to stop. Ever. Todd forced his mind back to the radio. "This late at night," he said, "the frequencies aren't as jammed as they are during the day. I think I fixed the wire that was loose in the back. Now, if I try every channel—"

"But it's almost midnight," Cassandra pointed out, "and you're exhausted. Why don't you come to bed?"

Todd shook his head. "We've got to keep trying," he said, covering a yawn. "It's our only chance." He spoke into the microphone again. "Come in, ski patrol. This is an S.O.S."

He nearly jumped out of his seat when a man's voice broke through the static. The voice was cracked and indistinct, but he was sure he heard someone say, "Is this Todd Wilkins?" He even thought he recognized a Southern accent.

"Yes!" he shouted. "This is Todd Wilkins! Is this the ski patrol?"

The man's voice responded, but Todd couldn't make out the words. Then he heard the softer sound of a woman's voice through the grating static.

"Elizabeth!" Todd yelled. He couldn't hear what she was saying, but he was sure that the voice was hers.

Now the man was speaking again. But again Todd couldn't understand his words.

"We're not hurt!" Todd told him, wanting to reassure Elizabeth. "But we're nearly out of food," he added. He hated to worry her any further, but the ski patrol had to know how desperate the situation was.

One phrase of the man's response was discernible in the static: "We've been trying to reach you, but we can't—" The static grew harsher until it filled the room.

Todd twisted the knob, but he couldn't bring back the voices. "We've lost the signal," he said hopelessly.

Cassandra's fingers dug deeper into his shoulder blades, smoothing out some of the tension. Todd took a deep breath and began to relax into the rhythm of her strokes. Then he shook his head, thinking of Elizabeth. He shrugged off Cassandra's hands, rose to his feet, and began to pace.

Jessica stopped pacing long enough to check the lighted numbers on the clock radio. "One in the morning!" she cried, standing in the middle of the room in her nightshirt, her hands on her hips. "Where is that girl?"

She stopped at the window and tried to peer outside. Her window was directly over the main entrance of the lodge, and she hoped to see Lila walking toward the front door. But frost covered the outside of the windowpane, making it difficult to see anything more than a vague impression of the snowy night outside. Jessica wrenched the window open a few inches and leaned her chin on the sill, ignoring the chill.

Under the dark sky, snow flurries fluttered softly to the ground. Jessica felt a pang of guilt. At the top of the mountain, she knew, the gentle snowfall was practically a blizzard, with near-zero temperatures and gale-force winds. And Elizabeth and Todd were both up there somewhere.

Well, I can't do anything about that now, she reminded herself. *So I might as well torture myself over Lila and Lucas instead.*

Suddenly, as if her words had conjured them up, Lila and Lucas appeared outside, strolling up the lighted path from the parking lot. Lila was holding Lucas's arm as if to keep from falling on the ice. And their laughter rang through the night.

Jessica watched as Lucas stopped in front of the door—directly under her window—and drew Lila closer to him. For a moment they gazed at each other as snowflakes whirled around them like a swarm of tiny butterflies. Lucas gently pushed back Lila's hood from her face. She rose up on tiptoe and wrapped her arms around his neck.

When their mouths met for a long, slow kiss, Jessica thought she was going to be sick. Lila had kissed Lucas first. She had won the bet.

Jessica pounded her fist against the wall, incensed. Then, on an impulse, she scooped up a handful of snow from the window ledge, took aim, and dropped it directly on Lila's smug, conceited head.

Chapter 11

Elizabeth stood in the doorway of the ski patrol station early Tuesday morning, hugging herself for warmth against the strong wind. The sky was gray and heavy with clouds. "It's not snowing nearly as hard as it was last night," she called over her shoulder to Dirk, who sat at the desk, leaning over the radio. "We'll be able to go out in the helicopter, won't we?"

Dirk shook his head. "Not yet," he said. "We can't take the chopper out in this wind."

"We have to!" Elizabeth insisted.

"I'm sorry, Liz," he said. "But if we try to pilot a helicopter in this wind, we're likely to crash into the side of the mountain. We'll have to wait until it dies down."

Elizabeth closed the door and stepped back inside.

"When will that be?" she asked glumly, sitting on the vinyl couch.

"I just spoke with a meteorologist at the National Weather Service," Dirk told her. "There's another blizzard headed straight for us this afternoon. But if we're lucky, the wind will die down for a while before the front comes through. That should give us a window of two or three hours to search."

Elizabeth leaned back against the couch cushions, staring at the ceiling. "Will that be enough time?" she asked quietly.

Dirk sat beside her. "It will have to be," he said. "I've narrowed the search down to the three cabins where Todd is most likely to be, given what you said about his last known location. We'll fly one pass over all three to see if we can make out any smoke coming from one of the chimneys. That way we won't waste time stopping somewhere where he isn't likely to be."

Elizabeth nodded. "Once the storm starts this afternoon, how long does the weather service think it will last?" she asked.

Dirk looked away from her. "The meteorologist's best estimate was three days," he said.

"And Todd said his food is running out," Elizabeth said faintly.

"Elizabeth," Dirk said, "even in our window of

opportunity, when the wind dies down today, this helicopter rescue is not going to be easy. Weather conditions are bad; we would never try to take a chopper out today if it weren't an emergency. Why don't you plan to wait here? I promise you that I will do everything humanly possible to get Todd out of there."

Elizabeth shook her head. "No!" she said. "I meant what I said last night. I'm coming with you."

Jessica sat in the chairlift next to Karen, trying to tune out the girl's perky banter about her complete lack of ability on the ski slopes. Instead Jessica's attention was focused on the couple in the seat just ahead of theirs. She gritted her teeth as Lila's blue hood leaned against Lucas's shoulder. She clenched her hands into fists as Lila's legs swung gently back and forth, rocking the seat with a light, rhythmic motion.

She knew that Lila was doing it all on purpose, just for Jessica's benefit. *It's her way of saying, "Ha, ha! He's mine!"* she mused darkly.

"I can't believe that Lucas is going to let me ski way up on the upper slopes!" Karen said. Jessica stifled the urge to stuff the girl's red tam into her constantly moving mouth. "I mean, I know we're not going all the way to the top, where the tram goes," Karen babbled on, "but it's higher than I've skied before. Of course, Lucas won't let me off the green runs. I'm still a complete klutz on skis—not like you and Lila. Lucas says you're both naturals. I guess you'll be skiing one of the steeper slopes."

"Devil's Run," Jessica said through her clenched teeth.

Karen's eyebrows shot up. "Devil's Run?" she asked. "But that's a double black diamond!"

Jessica shrugged. "So I've heard."

"You can't ski an experts-only slope!" Karen cried.

"Watch me," Jessica said. She wasn't afraid of Devil's Run—well, not exactly. She'd skied a black diamond run before. She wondered just how much harder a double black diamond could be. "I guess I might as well get it over with as soon as possible," she added under her breath. As soon as she reached the top of the ridge, she'd decided, she would head over to the most treacherous run on the mountain.

Enid's voice broke through her thoughts. "Jessica! There's a helicopter hovering around up there!" she called from a seat behind Jessica. "It must be the one that's going to rescue Todd."

Jessica craned her neck to see the top of the highest peak. Sure enough, a helicopter was buzzing over the summit. The wind buffeted it as it touched down somewhere behind the tram depot.

"Elizabeth's message this morning said she was going up with the ski patrol," Jessica called back to Enid and Winston. "I don't know about this. It doesn't look very safe."

"I'm sure the ski patrol wouldn't let her go along if there was any danger," Enid said bravely. But Jessica thought Enid sounded as unsure as Jessica herself felt. For a moment she wondered if she should call off her run down the mountain. It seemed disloyal, somehow, to worry about skiing when her sister was up in a helicopter that looked about as frail as a mosquito next to the bulk of the mountain and the looming snow clouds.

Jessica glanced ahead of her at Lila, who was whispering something into Lucas's ear. Instantly her resolve returned. If she begged off Devil's Run, Lila would say she was afraid. And there was nothing she could do for Elizabeth, anyway.

Besides, Lila's guard was down now that she was basking in her triumph over Jessica. Maybe there was still a way for Jessica to steal Lucas away. She stared thoughtfully at the back of her best friend's head. Lila may have won a major battle, she decided, but the war wasn't over yet.

Elizabeth's hair blew around her as the helicopter touched down on the pad a little before eleven o'clock Tuesday morning. She held on to her hat. It was still windy at the top of the mountain, and snow was falling. But Dirk said the wind had died down enough. If the ski patrol was going to search for Todd at all that day, now was the only possible time.

"Are you still resolved to do this?" Dirk asked, grasping Elizabeth's arm. He had to shout to be heard over the whirring of the helicopter blades.

Elizabeth nodded, not trusting her voice.

"All right," Dirk said into her ear. "You climb in first. I'll follow you with the other search-party members. But Elizabeth, I want you to remember that you're here as an observer, and that this trip could get dangerous. The weather may not look that bad right now. But in these mountains, a blizzard can appear out of nowhere. I need your promise that you'll do everything I tell you, without any argument. Is that clear?"

Elizabeth nodded again, biting her lip as if that could keep her fear in check. She had been sitting practically on top of the radio for two hours but had heard no further communications from Todd. And the weather service was still calling for a major storm that afternoon.

She looked east, toward the most rugged part of the mountain—the part where Todd was stranded. But visibility was poor, as though a giant gray cloud had descended from the sky and enveloped the top of the peak. She shuddered with more than the

191

cold. Then she took a deep, icy breath and climbed into the helicopter.

Lila rested an arm possessively around Lucas's waist as they balanced on their skis at the top of a high, gently sloping run. Now that she and Lucas were an item, she wanted everyone to know it. Especially Jessica. *That trick with the snowball last night was nasty,* Lila thought. *But what else should I expect from someone with Jessica's level of maturity?*

She glanced around, wondering where Jessica was. She'd noticed the way her best friend had glared at her on the chairlift a few minutes earlier. She was surprised that Jessica hadn't skied up and tried to come between Lila and Lucas. *Obviously,* Lila thought, *Jessica knows that she's lost this war.* Then she noticed Jessica's purple-and-pink-suited figure disappearing over a rise on the other side of the chairlift.

Good, she thought. *Jessica's heading over to Devil's Run to get her humiliation over with. This I have to see.* She couldn't tell Lucas about Devil's Run, of course. He would feel obligated to go after Jessica, to stop her. But surely she could find a way to lead him in that direction so that she could watch Jessica fall flat on her face.

"Where did Jessica run off to?" Lucas asked suddenly. "I swear, that girl is so unpredictable—"

"She's skiing Devil's Run," piped up Karen, who had just skied up from behind them.

Lucas whirled, nearly knocking Lila off balance. "Did you say Devil's Run?" he demanded.

"That's what she told me on the chairlift," Karen said.

"Damn!" Lucas cursed. "She's nowhere near ready for a double black diamond!"

Lila shrugged. "She'll be fine, Lucas," she said. "You told me yourself that you'd never seen someone improve so quickly."

"Lila, that run is more than just an advanced slope. It's restricted to experts only! And now that it's snowing again, the conditions will be even more dangerous." He pushed off and skied in the direction of Devil's Run. "I've got to stop her!" he called over his shoulder.

Lila tried to shoot icicles out of her eyes at Karen, who didn't seem to notice. The little twerp had wrecked everything by spilling the beans about Devil's Run. But it was Jessica who was really responsible, Lila decided. Jessica was always managing to find a way to come between her and Lucas.

Lila sighed loudly. Then she took off after Lucas. She wasn't going to give Jessica a chance to be alone with him—not even for a minute.

"That's it for the food," Cassandra said as she rinsed the metal plates in a bucket of melted snow.

193

"I guess you could call that our last supper. Or brunch, I suppose, since it's eleven in the morning."

Todd didn't answer. He scraped a thin film of ice from the inside of the cabin's small, high window and cupped his hand to peer through the frost that coated the outside of the pane. From inside the cabin, he had to stand on his toes to see out the window. But outside, the window was practically at ground level. "It's snowing again," he said finally. "And the sky is getting darker. I think we're in for a big storm."

"Oh, well," Cassandra said with strained-sounding cheerfulness. "At least we've got each other."

"That's about all we've got," Todd pointed out. He turned away from the window and dodged a trickle of water that was seeping through the roof. "We're just about out of firewood, and I couldn't find a single stick when I went out to search for more yesterday. If there are any trees on this part of the mountain, they're buried under a ton of snow and ice."

"Don't worry," Cassandra said. "The ski patrol knows we're out here. I'm sure they'll find us today."

"I don't think so," Todd said, rubbing his hand against his rough, unshaven chin. "I could've sworn that the guy on the radio said there was no way to reach us. And with a blizzard headed this way, there's no chance they'll be able to clear a path through to us today. It could be days before they find us."

"We're not really out of firewood," Cassandra pointed out. "We can burn the table if we have to. And the cabinets, and the other furniture. That would keep us going for another day."

"That's a good idea," Todd said reluctantly, wishing he had thought of it. "But there's something else we should be worried about."

Cassandra took one look at his troubled expression and her bravado dissipated. "Todd, what is it?" she asked.

He sighed. "See that leak in the roof?" he said, pointing to the trickle of water. "And that place over there, where water is running down the wall near the fireplace?"

"So the place leaks a little," Cassandra said. "A lot of old places do. We can put up with an occasional drop of melting snow."

Todd shook his head. "I wish that were all it was. But I think the problem is a lot more serious. Haven't you noticed the way the roof is sagging in the middle?" He pointed overhead, and Cassandra followed his gaze.

"Oh, no!" she exclaimed. "It *is* sagging. I'm sure it wasn't that bad when we first got here."

"And I don't know how to explain it," Todd continued, "but I just have this . . . *sense* that the snow overhead is getting too heavy for the structure. Don't you feel it, too?"

"Yeah," Cassandra admitted, sitting down limply on the couch. "It's like being claustrophobic—a feeling that the ceiling is slowly caving in on us."

Todd nodded, his sense of foreboding as heavy as the thick layer of snow on the cabin's roof. "And if it caves in before the ski patrol arrives," he concluded, "then we don't stand a chance of getting off this mountain alive."

Jessica slalomed down the first section of Devil's Run, glorying in the challenging descent and the fresh feel of the wind against her face. "Piece of cake," she said under her breath as she picked her line through a series of ice moguls and executed a perfect set of turns. Snow was falling more thickly now, limiting her visibility. And the packed surface was hard and slick.

The sky was still light at this elevation. But the storm was obviously much worse at the top of the mountain. Purple clouds were deepening on the edge of her peripheral vision. But for now, she felt in complete control as she flew down the run. Double black diamonds were no match for Jessica Wakefield.

Out of the corner of her eye, she saw Lucas approaching from one side, his red bandanna fluttering behind him as he glided expertly toward her. *What a body!* she thought immediately.

When it came right down to it, Jessica decided, one kiss didn't mean anything. Winning a silly bet wasn't important. The real prize was Lucas himself. And she still had a shot at him. Now that Lila was complacent, Jessica could move in for the kill. *But how would she get him alone?*

Suddenly Jessica felt her skis slice to one side. She'd been too busy thinking about Lucas to see the huge mogul in her path. Jessica lost control. Her head was thrown backward, and her body left the slope in a jump she hadn't anticipated and wasn't prepared for. The ridge spun around her, a kaleidoscope of snow, sky, and treetops. Then the mountainside loomed ahead, rushing toward her. She was going to hit it. She was going to crash.

Jessica opened her mouth to scream.

"The storm's ahead of schedule!" the helicopter pilot shouted back to Dirk. "I'm not sure how much longer we can stay in the air!"

"We have to!" Elizabeth screamed. "We've only flown over one of the cabins, and it didn't have any smoke!"

Dirk spoke into a headset, his voice unintelligible over the clatter of helicopter blades and the roar of the wind. Ominous clouds were amassing quickly, and the sky's strange light cast a purplish glow on the snowy mountainside below. The helicopter's insectlike shadow was still visible on the smooth blanket of snow beneath them, but just barely. It was only eleven thirty in the morning, but the sky was already growing dark. Elizabeth thought it looked more like dusk.

"The weather service says we're in for it any minute now!" Dirk announced. "What do you think, Henry?" he asked the pilot.

"This is your show," the pilot answered, "so it's your call. But if I get a vote, I say we take this baby down. Things are going to get real dicey up here, real soon."

The chopper was caught in an updraft, and Elizabeth felt her stomach lurch as the craft swooped up and then plummeted straight down for a split second.

"Sorry, Liz," Dirk shouted, "but it's too risky to stay up here. We'll have to head back! We'll try again when the weather clears."

Liz shook her head. "No!" she screamed, sobbing. "Please, Dirk! Todd will die if we don't reach him soon. I know he will!"

Dirk conferred with the pilot. Then he turned back to Elizabeth with a sigh. "All right," he told her reluctantly. "We'll stay up a little while longer. But that storm will be slamming into us soon, full force. There's no way of knowing when. It could be minutes from now, or it could be hours. But the moment it hits—Todd or no Todd—we're heading back to the helipad." He paused and took a deep breath. "Assuming we have time to get to it."

Jessica had no idea which way was up. She had no sense of time or place. All she knew was that her body was tumbling, with no more control than a rag doll. And the mountainside was rushing at her, immense and unstoppable.

Out of the corner of her eye, she saw the flash of a red bandanna. Lucas was hurtling toward her. She had a momentary impression of his handsome features, etched with fear. Then she slammed into him with an impact that sent both of them skidding down the ridge.

Dirk pointed to the mountainside below, and Elizabeth gasped when she saw the wide swath of destruction the avalanche had blazed down the side of the mountain. *Nobody could survive something so enormous and terrible,* she thought, choked with panic. For a moment she was sure she was going to throw up.

"There!" Dirk shouted suddenly. "The cabin

must be completely buried. But a stream of smoke is rising from that bank!"

Elizabeth's nausea vanished. "That must be Todd!" she cried. "It has to be!"

"We'll have to dig our way down to the door once we reach the cabin," Dirk said to the two other ski patrol members who were part of the rescue team. "Be ready with the proper equipment. We'll have to work fast."

"I see a place where we can put the chopper down, not far from that bank," the pilot shouted over the sound of the motor. "And hurry with this rescue, or we won't get this baby back up again. The wind is rising."

The helicopter rocked from side to side as it descended toward the high, barren plain of snow. Elizabeth fell against Dirk, and he wrapped an arm around her shoulders to steady her. Suddenly the helicopter dropped precipitously. Elizabeth screamed as the mountain rushed toward her. But Henry regained control, and the craft jerked upward with a shudder that reverberated through Elizabeth's body. She hid her face against Dirk's shoulder. Then, slowly, the helicopter descended, in a series of lurches that tied Elizabeth's stomach in knots.

"Why don't you stay here in the helicopter, Liz?" Dirk asked gently when the helicopter was finally on solid ground. "It'll be rough going out there, and this won't take long."

Elizabeth shook her head. "No!" she choked out. "I'm coming with you."

"I had a feeling you'd say that," Dirk said, squeezing her shoulders. "You know, you've got a lot of courage."

Elizabeth looked up at him gratefully. Then she followed him out of the helicopter and began slogging her way through the deep, deep snow.

The cabin's one high window was dark now. And Todd could no longer hear the rush of wind and snow outside. He walked slowly to the center of the room. "The snow must be piled up past the walls," he told Cassandra, who was standing near the fireplace, warming her hands in front of the tiny fire they'd allowed themselves. "We're completely buried."

A loud creak erupted from one corner of the roof. Todd's eyes widened in terror. But the roof held.

Cassandra bit her lip. "I'm scared, Todd," she said helplessly. "I'm really scared."

She walked up behind him and put her arms around him. Todd felt the front of her body against his back and pulled away.

"Please hug me," she begged. "Just hug me." Even in the dimness of the cabin, he could see tears glistening in her eyes. He reached out and held her tightly, closing his eyes as if that could keep him from hearing the noises that could only mean the imminent collapse of the cabin around them. The grating sounds had begun overhead but now seemed to be mocking them from the walls as well. Todd had never been so frightened.

Cassandra's lips brushed against the side of his face and then sought out his mouth. Todd's eyes flew open, and he tried to turn his head away from her.

Elizabeth was the only one in the rescue party who wasn't weighed down with digging equipment. As soon as Dirk's rescue party had dug a deep enough hole by the door of the cabin, she leaped down into it and pushed open the door. She rushed into the cold, dim cabin, feeling Dirk's solid presence at her back.

"Todd!" she cried. Then she felt her face go dead white. Todd stood in the center of the room, his arms around a shapely older woman, his lips against hers.

"Elizabeth!" he exclaimed as his own face turned red.

Elizabeth shook her head in disbelief. All this time, she had been worried sick about him. And he had been here with that . . . woman. She spun and ran out the door into the blinding storm.

Chapter 12

"Elizabeth!" Todd called, hurrying out the door of the cabin after her. But she couldn't stop to talk to him. She couldn't even bear to look at him.

Outside the cabin, she scrambled to the surface of the snow and began stumbling toward the helicopter, only vaguely noticing that the full force of the storm had hit at last.

She felt a hand on her shoulder. "Elizabeth!" Todd screamed over the howling wind. "It wasn't what it looked like. Please! You have to listen to me!"

Elizabeth shook her head and pushed his hand away. When she climbed into the helicopter a few minutes later, she chose a seat up front, near the pilot. She knew there would be no room there for Todd to get close to her.

"We'll never be able to land on the summit in

this storm!" she vaguely heard the pilot shout. "I'm taking us all the way down the mountain to the helipad behind the lodge. Hang on, everyone!" he warned. "We're in for a dangerous trip!"

Elizabeth didn't say a word on the entire flight back. She only stared out the window at the whirling snow, too numb to feel more than a vague sense of terror.

When the helicopter finally landed, Elizabeth was relieved to hear that Todd would be busy for the next couple of hours. First he would be examined by a doctor at the resort's clinic to make sure he hadn't injured himself when he fell. After that, the head of the ski patrol's main office wanted a report from both Todd and the woman in red about exactly what had happened to them. She sighed gratefully. She didn't think she would be able to face Todd for some time.

Todd walked toward the ski patrol office, looking back in an effort to catch her eye. Elizabeth refused to glance up. She stumbled out of the helicopter, nearly blinded by her tears. But she refused to cry in front of everyone. She absolutely would not.

She felt a hand on her elbow, and then Dirk pulled her close, his face full of sympathy. "You're ten times more beautiful than she is," he whispered into her ear. She blinked back her tears and gazed gratefully into his eyes. Then she pulled away and ran inside, to the privacy of her room.

Lila sat beside Lucas's bed in Snow Mountain's two-room clinic. "Does your ankle hurt?" she asked, brushing a lock of thick black hair from his eyes.

"It's not too bad," Lucas replied, staring ruefully at his foot. "The doctor says it's only a sprain. I got off lucky, compared to Jessica," he added. "Her ankle is fractured."

"It's her own fault, for trying to ski down a run she wasn't ready for," Lila said. "I don't know what got into her!"

The door swung open, and Jessica entered the room, steering a wheelchair toward them. "I just got word from Ms. Jacobi at the lodge," she said. "The ski patrol found Todd and the other person he was stranded with," she announced. "Liz is back, too, and everyone's OK."

Lucas looked confused. "Who are Todd and Liz?" he asked.

Jessica and Lila looked at each other and shook their heads at the same time. "It's a long story," Jessica said. "Remind me to tell you about it some other time. And we'll have *lots* of time in the next few days as we recover together. But don't worry. I'll take care of you, Lucas."

Lila rolled her eyes. As usual, Jessica was trying

to horn in on her conquest. And this time she was being unrealistic in more ways than one. "Jess, you can't even take care of yourself," she reminded her, pointing to the cast on Jessica's leg. "*I'll* take care of Lucas."

"Thanks for your concern, girls," Lucas interjected. "But I think I can manage to take care of myself. I will be staying at the hotel, though, at least for the next few days. The lodge has offered me a suite so that I can be close to the clinic until my ankle is a little better."

Lila smiled broadly. Lucas was acting a little distant now. But he would be nearby twenty-four hours a day. She was sure she could get him to warm up to her again. Certainly Jessica was in no condition to put up much of a pursuit.

At nine o'clock that evening, Jessica hopped on her good leg from the bathroom to the bed. The impact of every hop jarred her injured ankle painfully. But the wheelchair had only been for use at the clinic. And her new crutches were even more awkward than hopping.

"How is Liz?" Lila asked, her tone polite rather than genuinely concerned.

Jessica shrugged. "Very un-Liz-like," she said. "I thought she would be all worried about my death-defying experience today—"

206

"Come off it, Jessica," Lila interrupted sharply. "You have a hairline fracture in your ankle. It's not as if you almost died or anything."

"That's easy for you to say!" Jessica complained. "You're just mad because Lucas risked his life to save me."

"Did I say you weren't badly injured?" Lila asked. "I stand corrected. You obviously suffered serious *brain damage*. At least you didn't hurt anything *important*—"

"As I was saying," Jessica continued, speaking over Lila's remark, "Elizabeth hardly seemed to notice that I could have been killed today. I guess she was still upset about Todd. The funny thing was that she wasn't even with him! I figured they'd be even more attached at the hip than usual, after what they've been through this week."

Lila shrugged. "I don't know what the big mystery is," she said impatiently. "Todd didn't get to eat or sleep much during the whole time he was out there, let alone shower. I mean, give the guy a break! He was probably exhausted and went straight to his room to order room service."

"I guess," Jessica said. "But there's no need to get snooty about it." She arranged her leg on the bed with some difficulty, but her mind was on Lucas. She still meant to steal him away from Lila, but she couldn't figure out how. Suddenly something clicked in her mind. She remembered one of Elizabeth's favorite big-sisterly lectures—the one about how friends should stick together and not fight over a guy. She thought it through and decided that it just might work.

"Gosh, Lila," she said suddenly, inflecting her voice with just the right amount of sincere remorse. "This is stupid!"

"What's stupid?" Lila asked, suspicious.

Jessica shook her head. "You and I, sniping at each other like this. I'm sorry. But it's been a really rotten week. Lucas decided he liked you better than me. And Elizabeth has been freaking out. And now my ankle hurts awfully. . . ." She managed to summon up a single teardrop.

"Jessica, what are you saying?" Lila asked.

"I'm not sure," Jessica said in a resigned tone. "I guess I'm tired of us being mad at each other. You're my best friend, and Lucas is just a ski bum that we'll probably never see again after next weekend. Can't we just decide that our friendship is more important than some guy?"

Lila sighed. "You're right," she agreed. "I can't believe it took an accident like this to get us to see what we've been doing to our friendship."

"How about a deal?" Jessica proposed. "We shake hands and agree that neither one of us will try to get romantic with Lucas again." She held out her right hand and shook Lila's with a tearful smile.

But behind Jessica's back, the fingers of her left hand were tightly crossed.

"I feel so much better now that we're friends again," Lila said as she shook Jessica's hand. "Enid and Elizabeth were right last week when they said that we're too competitive with each other. I'm glad that phase of our friendship is over!"

Lila's voice rang with sincerity. But she smiled to herself as she crossed her fingers behind her back.

Later that night, Elizabeth sat on one of the overstuffed couches in the lodge's lobby, staring into the fire. She was glad that the rest of her schoolmates had gone to bed early after the eventful day. She didn't want to talk to any of them. She couldn't bear having them know about Todd and the woman in the red snowsuit.

To her dismay, she felt somebody sit down beside her. She turned to tell Todd to go away. To her surprise, she was staring into Dirk's warm hazel eyes.

"How are you doing?" he asked in his soft drawl.

Elizabeth looked down at her hands. She took a deep breath. Dirk was the only other person who had seen what she'd seen in that cabin. He was the only one who knew about her loss and her humiliation. "I don't know," she said in a small, helpless voice. "I don't understand how he could do that to me."

Dirk patted her back sympathetically as she poured out her feelings—her love for Todd, their long-standing relationship, and their recent disagreements. "I knew we were having some problems in the last week," she concluded. "I mean, he was acting so differently! But I had no idea he wanted to be with somebody else. I never thought Todd would do that!"

"I know," Dirk said, beginning to massage her neck. "And it's even more of a betrayal after what you've been through in the last few days. You risked your life for him."

Elizabeth closed her eyes and relaxed into the warmth of his sympathy. Suddenly she was shocked to feel Dirk's lips against hers. She was angry at Todd, but she was still in love with him. Kissing another man wouldn't be right, no matter what Todd had done to her. She pushed her hands against Dirk's chest, but he only held her tighter.

"Todd doesn't deserve you," Dirk whispered into her ear.

Elizabeth heard a gasp. She looked over Dirk's shoulder into Todd's anguished face.

"Elizabeth!" Todd exploded. "I can't believe this! Just a few hours ago you were accusing me, but—"

"No, Todd!" she cried. "It's not like that!"

"—all along," he continued, "you were the one

210

who was two-timing me, even while I was stranded out there!"

He stomped away, furious. And Elizabeth's eyes filled with tears.

Jessica pretended to be just opening her eyes when Lila emerged from the bathroom the next morning. She moaned slightly.

"Are you all right?" Lila asked.

Jessica nodded. "Yes, I'm fine. I just turned my leg in the wrong direction," she said, wincing. "You know, I'm really feeling pretty ragged this morning. My ankle hurts, and I'm sore all over from wiping out yesterday. Maybe I'll just stay in bed and see what's on pay-per-view."

"Do you want me to stay with you?" Lila asked.

Jessica waved her hand. "Oh, no!" she said. "You go ahead and have some fun. Maybe you can meet some guys for us."

"All right," Lila agreed. "I can at least get in a few hours of skiing before Winston's Welcome-Back Party, the Sequel. He said three o'clock, didn't he?"

"Is the weather OK for skiing today?" Jessica asked.

"I just heard a weather report," Lila said. "It's still stormy on the top of the mountain, but the lower slopes are fine."

As soon as Lila was gone, Jessica jumped out of bed and hopped to the bathroom to spiff up her hair and makeup. She was aiming for a slightly pale, delicate, and completely un-made-up look. After a half hour, she thought she had it. Her tight jeans wouldn't fit over the cast on her ankle. So she pulled on a clingy red sweater dress, reached for her crutches, and made her way to Lucas's suite.

"Come in! The door's open!" he called in response to her knock.

Jessica hobbled into the room. Lucas sat on a couch in front of a roaring fire, his ankle propped up on a coffee table. Jessica sighed. Soft music was playing in the background, and Lucas wore a navy-and-green sweater that made his shoulders look incredibly broad. Everything was perfect.

"All of my friends have abandoned me," she said in a small voice. "Do you mind if I hang out with you?"

"Of course not," he said with a grin. "But excuse me if I don't get up."

An hour later Lila stepped into the ski lodge. She'd taken one good run on the mountain, and that was plenty. Jessica wasn't expecting her back for hours. She had plenty of time to sneak up to Lucas's room. What Jessica didn't know wouldn't hurt her.

As she passed her room, Lila noticed that the door wasn't completely shut. She stood in the hallway outside and peered in, expecting to see Jessica propped up in bed, watching television. But the bed was empty. Lila was furious. She ran into the room and made a quick survey of it. Jessica was gone, all right. And Lila knew exactly where she was. So much for Jessica's sad-eyed can't-we-be-friends-again speech.

Lila stormed out of the room and headed down the hall toward Lucas's suite. Jessica was about to learn the error of her ways.

Chapter 13

Elizabeth and Enid had decided to splurge and order room service for lunch. Elizabeth was obviously afraid of running into Todd in the restaurant. And Enid was so discouraged by her own prospects for romance that she was considering remaining in their room for the rest of the week. So instead of venturing out of their room, they sat cross-legged on the bed, eating sandwiches.

"No!" Elizabeth said again. "I don't want to talk about Todd. I told you what happened, and there's nothing else to say. He thinks I'm two-timing him, and he doesn't trust me enough to listen to what really happened with Dirk last night!"

"But Elizabeth—" Enid began.

"Please, Enid," Elizabeth begged. "Let's talk about something else. Tell me what you've been doing the past few days. I swear, we've hardly seen each other at all."

Enid rolled her eyes. "You wouldn't believe it if I told you," she said, gesturing with a pickle.

"Try me."

Enid reached over to yank open the drawer of her bedside table. "Here's what I've been doing all this time," she said, pulling out the little book and tossing it to Elizabeth.

Elizabeth's mouth dropped open. "*A Hundred and One Ways to Be Sassy on the Slopes,*" she read aloud. "Enid Rollins, I never would have believed it if you hadn't told me yourself! What's this all about?"

"I was determined to have a romantic fling this week," Enid said. "The woman in the bookstore guaranteed that this book would help me find romance."

"Did it?" Elizabeth asked.

"Well, I'm sitting here scarfing down sandwiches with you," Enid pointed out, laughing, "instead of gazing over a candlelit table into the eyes of some hunky ski bum. So obviously it didn't work."

"Fluorescent zinc oxide?" Elizabeth asked, leafing through the book. "You can't be serious! That doesn't sound like your style!"

Enid smiled. "Are you kidding? The guy I picked up because of my lime green nose said I had lots of style."

"You actually picked up a guy that way?"

"Sure," Enid said. "But I threw him back. I'm not sure if it was the nose ring or the green ponytail."

Elizabeth erupted into laughter. "This is just too good!" she cried. "Tell me more!"

"Last night I tried the one where you find a group of good-looking guys and ask directions to the hot tub—Method Twenty-six, if I remember correctly."

Elizabeth thumbed to the right page. "It says here that one of the guys will invariably offer to personally escort you to the hot tub. Did you get an invitation?"

"No," Enid said. "All I got were directions to the hot tub. But the directions were screwed up, and I ended up in the laundry room instead."

"Method Twenty-nine is to hang out in the laundry room and offer to help guys sort their whites from their colors," Elizabeth pointed out. "Did you try that one, as long as you were there?"

Enid nodded. "Yep," she said. "There was a huge, muscle-bound type in there. In fact, I think it was the same guy Jess and Lila were making eyes at a few days ago, in that diner near Grand Junction."

Elizabeth's eyes widened. "You're kidding!" she exclaimed. "Did he let you handle his whites for him?"

"He sure did," she said. "Little tiny T-shirts and

216

onesies. Eighteen-month-old size. The guy is married, with a baby!"

Elizabeth giggled and turned back to the book. "Snowboarding!" she cried. "Oh, Enid. You didn't!"

"I did," Enid said proudly. "And I lived to tell the tale. Unfortunately, the only guy there who showed any interest was the Green Ponytail Dude again. Luckily, by then he thought Winston would rip out his nose ring if he laid a hand on me."

"Winston?"

"It's a long story," Enid admitted. "But believe it or not, Winston was helping me out in my, uh, romantic endeavors this week." Her voice turned serious. "Honestly, Liz, even though nothing worked out in the end, I don't know what I would have done without him. He kept me from getting too discouraged."

Elizabeth's voice grew serious, too. "Too bad I didn't have him up on the mountain with me," she said. "Or in front of the fireplace last night."

"Liz, I know you don't want to hear this," Enid said hesitantly, "but Todd might have a perfectly reasonable explanation for what you thought you saw in that cabin."

"Reasonable explanation?" Elizabeth fumed. "What possible explanation can there be? I was frantic, thinking he was in danger. And the whole time he was making out with a sexy older woman in a secluded cabin in the middle of nowhere! I know what I saw, and it was a definite, serious kiss."

"It sounds a lot like what Todd saw in front of the fireplace," Enid said quietly.

Elizabeth's mouth dropped open. "Oh," she exclaimed, realization dawning in her eyes. "You're absolutely right. I'm doing the same thing to Todd that I was accusing him of doing to me. And both of us are so sure that the other is cheating that we refuse to even listen to the other side of the story."

Enid nodded. "That's how it looks from where I sit," she said. "You two love each other, Liz. You were telling me the other day that your relationship is built on trust. . . ."

"But we didn't trust each other enough to sit down and talk about it," Elizabeth said.

"Does this mean you plan to talk to him now?" Enid asked.

"Yes," Elizabeth said. "It's the only way we'll ever find out what really happened. Thanks, Enid. You've been a big help."

"That's me," Enid said. "I'm great at advising everyone else what to do with their love life. But when it comes to having one of my own . . ." Her voice trailed off.

"When it comes to having one of your own," Elizabeth said, flipping through the book again, "I want you to try Method One Hundred and One."

"No way!" Enid said. "I've had it with that book. I'm resigning myself to sitting single on the chairlift."

Elizabeth smiled. "Just try this one method," she pleaded. "Come on, do it as a favor to me."

"OK, OK," Enid said, rolling her eyes. "What's Method One Hundred and One?"

"I'll read it to you," Elizabeth said. "Here goes: 'Do what makes you happy,'" she read. "'Think about what you would most like to be doing right now. And then do it—whether it's slaloming down a tricky run, sitting in the hotel pool, or treating yourself to a nice dinner in the restaurant. Don't worry about impressing anyone. Just be yourself. You never know when you'll run into a handsome guy who's chosen the same activity.'"

Enid took the book from her. "Let me see that," she said thoughtfully, rereading the passage. "You know, that sounds like good advice."

"So what would make you happy right now?" Elizabeth asked.

"Marshmallows," Enid said instantly.

"What?"

"Every time I walk by that big fireplace downstairs, I'm dying to toast marshmallows," Enid explained. "Winston gave me the idea the other night. And ever since then, I've been promising myself that I would do it. Now I think I will—on one condition."

"What's that?" Elizabeth asked.

"You have to talk to Todd and straighten things out between the two of you."

Elizabeth hugged her gratefully. "It's a deal," she agreed.

Jessica leaned against Lucas's shoulder, snuggling into his soft wool sweater as they sat on the couch in front of the fireplace.

"This is really nice," she murmured into his ear. "I never knew there were such advantages to being injured."

She gazed into his brilliant blue eyes and felt something melt inside her. Finally the time was right. She leaned in closer, and their lips met in a soft, sensuous kiss. Jessica was sure she was in heaven.

A banging on the door interrupted her reverie. "Who in the world could that be?" she asked. Suddenly she was afraid she knew the answer. "I'll get the door!" she said quickly. "You stay right there and remember where we left off."

She grabbed her crutches and used them to pull herself to her feet. Then she hobbled across the room to the door. Before she opened it, she fastened the chain lock.

Lila's angry brown eyes peered through the crack in the door. "Jessica Wakefield, you let me in this instant!" she hissed.

Jessica glared at her for a moment. Then she pushed the door shut and locked it.

"Who was that?" Lucas called as she returned to their spot in front of the fireplace.

"Nobody," Jessica said, leaning her crutches against the couch and sitting back down beside him. "It was just some girl looking for someone," she explained. "But she had the wrong room."

Minutes later, Lila held out a fifty-dollar bill in front of a bellhop who was a couple of years younger than herself. "Now, do you understand the plan?" she asked.

The boy nodded.

"And you'll do everything exactly the way I say?"

"Yes, ma'am," he averred. Lila narrowed her eyes at being called "ma'am" but decided to let it slide. She handed him the fifty-dollar bill. "Then let's get on with it," she said. "And hurry."

Jessica ran her fingers through Lucas's thick black hair. "Your aftershave smells great," she told him in a breathy voice. He turned toward her and leaned in for another kiss.

Before he reached her lips, a rapping sounded

on the door. Jessica groaned. Lila's timing left a lot to be desired. "Let's ignore it," she said. "It's probably another mixed-up person looking for somebody else's room."

"Room service!" called a male voice from outside the door.

"Did you order anything?" she asked Lucas.

"Not me," he said.

"Lunch for two for Mr. Lucas King," called the voice outside the door. "Compliments of the management, in regret for his injury in the line of duty."

Jessica grinned. Now they could stay together in Lucas's room all day long. They wouldn't even have to go downstairs for lunch. "Just a minute!" she called as she reached for her crutches. She limped to the door and opened it tentatively. A boy of fourteen or fifteen was standing in the hallway next to a white-skirted cart with silver serving pieces on top. She hurriedly unlatched the chain and ushered him in.

"I'm going to freshen up before lunch," she told Lucas as the boy from room service set about positioning the cart near the couch. She smiled to herself as she heard the boy shut the door behind him. Once again she was alone with Lucas in his luxurious suite. And they were about to eat a delicious, free lunch before getting back to the serious business of kissing on the couch.

"It doesn't get any better than this," she said under her breath, looking back at Lucas's broad shoulders and narrow hips. She scooted into the bathroom and shut the door behind her.

As soon as Lila heard the bathroom door shut behind Jessica, she jumped out from under the white-skirted room-service cart. She noticed that Lucas nearly fell off the couch at her sudden appearance. Silently she scrambled across the room and wedged a chair under the bathroom doorknob. Then she plopped down next to Lucas on the couch.

"Happy to see me?" she asked, cuddling up to him.

Lucas was speechless.

Jessica, naturally, was not. "What the heck is going on?" Jessica demanded through the bathroom door. "Lucas, I can't open this door."

"Too bad it isn't your mouth!" Lila called.

"Lila!" Jessica screamed. "You rotten creep! You let me out of here this instant!"

"Why would I want to do a stupid thing like that?" Lila yelled back.

Jessica sounded outraged. "How dare you lock me in here!"

"Lila," Lucas interrupted, "I haven't the faintest idea what's happening here, or why. But I wish you would let Jessica out of the bathroom."

Lila smiled sweetly at him. "Of course, Lucas," she said. "Anything for you."

As soon as the door was unblocked, Jessica hopped out on one foot, her crutches forgotten. "I can't believe you would do such a crummy, deceitful thing—" she began.

"*I'm* deceitful?" Lila asked, her voice rising to a high pitch. "Me? You're the one who said you'd be in our room all day, watching pay-per-view! After you agreed that neither one of us would go after Lucas!"

Lucas's eyes popped open. "Now, wait a minute, girls," he said, reaching for his own crutches and rising to his feet. "I'm not sure—"

"Whatever happened to no more competition between us?" Jessica screeched at Lila. "You said you wanted to be friends again!"

"And you said our friendship was more important than some ski bum!" Lila shot back.

Jessica, standing on one foot, nearly lost her balance. "At least I'm too mature to resort to locking people in the bathroom!"

"Mature?" Lila laughed. "You? You're about as mature as the average six-year-old! What kind of dope risks her life on a dangerous ski run over some guy she barely knows?"

"And what kind of manipulative brat suggests it in the first place?" Jessica yelled.

"Don't listen to her, Lucas," Lila said. "Devil's Run was all Jessica's idea—" She stopped, flustered. Lucas was nowhere to be seen.

Todd sat on the window seat in the hotel's lounge, just off the lobby. Behind him, Winston was blowing up balloons.

"One more hour," Winston promised between breaths, "and you are going to be the proud recipient of the best welcome-back party ever seen in these parts! I'm calling it Welcome-Back Party, the Sequel."

"I don't know, Winston," Todd said glumly.

"All right, if you don't like that, we'll call it Welcome-Back Party, Part Two," Winston suggested.

"It's not that," Todd said.

"Son of Welcome-Back Party?"

"Winston—" Todd began in a threatening tone.

"OK, OK," Winston said. "Excuse me for trying to cheer you up. But maybe you're being too hard on Liz. Maybe—"

Todd turned to stare at his friend. "Too hard on her? Winston, I guess I didn't make myself clear. Elizabeth was sitting in front of the fire, sharing a passionate kiss with some ski patrol guy. I hear she even spent the last two nights up on top of the mountain, in his office!"

"That's right," Winston said. "She wanted to be close to the radio in case you got a message

225

through. Wilkins, she was frantic about you! And from what I hear, she spent those nights up there *alone*. Dirk what's-his-name wasn't there with her."

"I don't know, Winston," Todd said, more depressed and confused than he'd ever been. "I think I need to be alone for a few minutes. Would you mind giving me some space right now? You've still got almost an hour to blow up balloons."

Winston bowed deeply. "Your wish is my command," he said. "I'll go check on the food."

Todd turned to the window, which looked toward the ski areas. From his seat he had a perfect view of the path from the slopes. He half expected to see Elizabeth walking up it, arm in arm with that guy from the ski patrol.

He sighed. He had to face facts. He had pushed Elizabeth too hard—first on the bus, and then in his room Saturday night. Now he had lost her—and to a guy named *Dirk!* "Oh, well," he said under his breath, "if I get lonely, there's always Cassandra."

He shook his head at the thought of the sexy but overbearing woman in the red snowsuit. Two days alone with her had been about as much as he could take.

Suddenly somebody grabbed him from behind. A woman's fingers covered his eyes. *Oh, no,* he thought. *Speak of the devil.* It could only be Cassandra.

He turned to tell her politely that she'd already

caused enough trouble for him. His heart soared. Elizabeth was standing there, a tentative but hopeful smile on her face. "Todd?" she asked. "Can we talk?"

Todd grinned. "Can we ever!" he exclaimed.

"I just wanted to apologize—" she began.

"Don't apologize!" he interrupted. "I'm the one who should apologize!"

"But I wouldn't listen when you—" she said.

"Neither would I," he replied.

"I swear, Todd, I was not two-timing you," Elizabeth said earnestly. She was staring him straight in the eye, and Todd knew her well enough to know that she was speaking the truth. "Dirk helped me a lot those two days. He was a good friend, and I'm grateful to him. But I guess I gave him the wrong idea. Todd, he was kissing me. I was not kissing him."

Todd grinned. "That's exactly what happened with Cassandra," he said. "Except that she was coming on to me from the moment I met her," he admitted. "I have to admit that I was flattered. But I never was really interested. I kept comparing her to you, and I couldn't see the point."

"Todd, about Saturday night—" Elizabeth began.

"Don't," he said. "I was wrong to push it, and I'm sorry."

"You know how much I love you," Elizabeth said.

"Remind me," he suggested, taking her in his arms.

227

"Next time," Elizabeth murmured, gazing into his eyes, "let's have a little more faith in each other. Things aren't always what they seem."

Todd stared at her silky blond hair and her shining blue-green eyes. Then he leaned in for a tender, passionate kiss.

"Welcome back," she whispered.

A minute later their embrace was interrupted by the sound of a man clearing his throat. Elizabeth turned, blushing, to the archway that led to the hotel lobby. Her eyes opened wide when she saw who was there.

Dirk and Cassandra stood in the entrance, looking as if they were glued to each other. They both seemed relieved to see Elizabeth and Todd so obviously together.

Cassandra smiled. "Sorry about the misunderstanding earlier," she said to Elizabeth. "I thought Todd was a big boy."

Dirk, at least, had the grace to look embarrassed. "If you don't mind," he said, "we've decided that, uh, under the circumstances it would be better if we skipped the welcome-back party."

"No problem," Todd said quickly, his brown eyes twinkling.

Dirk and Cassandra disappeared toward the elevator, and Elizabeth and Todd turned to each other.

"Did that really happen?" Elizabeth asked. "Or did I imagine the whole scene?"

"I'm more interested in what was happening a few minutes earlier," Todd admitted, wrapping his arms around her again. "Now, where were we?"

It was three o'clock, time for Winston's second try at a welcome-back party for Todd. Jessica didn't feel much like partying. But she'd already invited Lucas to the party, and she couldn't risk staying away and allowing Lila a chance to be alone with him.

She almost laughed out loud at how ludicrous the thought was. Lucas had heard her and Lila screaming like banshees at each other—not to mention practically admitting that they'd been using him like a prize in a game show. After that, she'd be shocked if the ski instructor ever wanted to see either one of them again.

"You really loused this week up for us both," Lila said to her as they stepped out of the elevator together. Lila was carrying on the same argument they'd begun upstairs, but her voice had lost its edge. Jessica suspected that Lila was also beginning to see the uselessness of continuing the warfare.

"I didn't louse up anything," Jessica replied halfheartedly, maneuvering her crutches onto the rug in the lobby. "You're the one who—"

She looked up, toward the fireplace, and nearly fell off her crutches.

Lila's gaze followed her wide-eyed stare. "Tell me the truth," Lila said incredulously after a long moment. "We're both dreaming, right? We don't see what I think we see."

Jessica stared at the couple who sat on the lumpy, overstuffed sofa in front of the fireplace. "Mass hallucination, I'd guess," she said slowly. "It has to be."

But it was no hallucination. Lucas sat on the couch, his arm around a girl with wavy reddish-brown hair. And he was gazing at her face as if they were the only two people in the world. The girl was Enid Rollins.

As Jessica and Lila watched from across the room, Enid slipped a toasted marshmallow off a stick and placed it delicately onto Lucas's tongue. Neither of the two on the couch noticed their audience.

Jessica and Lila stared at each other, amazed.

"Enid?" Jessica asked, shaking her head. "Lucas passed up a chance at both of us—for *Enid*?"

Lila's shoulders slumped. "This is the most humiliating thing that's ever happened to us," she wailed.

"That's for sure," Jessica agreed as they walked on, toward the lounge off to one side of the lobby. It took her a moment to realize that Lila had said "us." Jessica grinned.

"So what are we going to do about Enid and Lucas?" Lila asked, taking Jessica's arm to steady her when one of the crutches caught on a piece of furniture.

"The only thing we can do," Jessica said thoughtfully. "We're going to go in there to Winston's party, and we're going to welcome Todd back from his igloo," she announced. "And then we're going to have a terrific time," she added. "*After* we tell everyone in sight that *we* dumped Lucas first!"

Jessica and Lila looked at each other again and erupted in laughter. It was good to be friends again.

Bantam Books in the Sweet Valley High series.

Ask your bookseller for the books you have missed.

We hope you enjoyed reading this book. If you would like to receive further information about available titles in the Bantam series, just write to the address below, with your name and address:

KIM PRIOR
Bantam Books
61–63 Uxbridge Road
London W5 5SA

If you live in Australia or New Zealand and would like more information about the series, please write to:

SALLY PORTER
Transworld Publishers (Australia) Pty Ltd
15–25 Helles Avenue
Moorebank
NSW 2170
AUSTRALIA

KIRI MARTIN
Transworld Publishers (NZ) Ltd
3 William Pickering Drive
Albany
Auckland
NEW ZEALAND

All Transworld titles are available by post from:

Book Service By Post, PO Box 29,
Douglas, Isle of Man IM99 1BQ

Credit cards accepted.
Please telephone 01624 675137, fax 01624 670923
or Internet http://www.bookpost.co.uk for details

Please allow for post and packing:

UK: £0.75 per book
Overseas: £1.00 per book